"This is your idea of a date?"

Hank looked around the *Gazette*'s office. He had been hoping for a more *intimate* setting.

"I thought if I gave you the grand tour, you'd accept my career." Susan wanted Hank to understand—otherwise, there would be no hope for a reconciliation.

"I'm damned proud of what you do. What do you think attracted me in the first place?"

"I've always wondered," Susan admitted. "Why did you ask me to that dance?"

"There was a sense of purpose about you." Hank shrugged self-consciously. "I guess I was hoping some of it would rub off on me."

"Incredible. There I was, worrying about the loveless fate of girls who wear glasses, and a football player actually asked me out because he respected my brain."

"Why did you say yes?" Hank moved in closer. This was more the kind of date he had imagined.

"I thought you were sexy."

Hank grinned and waited for her to elaborate. When she didn't, his smile slid into an incredulous gape. "That's it? You thought I was sexy?"

"Still do," she whispered huskily.

An Imperfect Hero is set in the Delta region of Arkansas where author **Jo Morrison** grew up. People still tend to marry young in this rural farming community. Jo has observed the special bond that exists between those husbands and wives who both grow up and grow old together. She wanted to write *An Imperfect Hero* to honor those couples who are able to fall in love over and over again with each other.

Hank and Susan Metcalf, the hero and heroine, were introduced as minor characters in Jo's first Temptation novel, *Always* (#312), which was nominated as Best First Novel by the Romance Writers of America.

Books by Jo Morrison

HARLEQUIN TEMPTATION
312—ALWAYS

Don't miss any of our special offers. Write to us at the following address for information on our newest releases.

Harlequin Reader Service
P.O. Box 1397, Buffalo, NY 14240
Canadian address: P.O. Box 603,
Fort Erie, Ont. L2A 5X3

An Imperfect Hero

JO MORRISON

Harlequin Books

TORONTO • NEW YORK • LONDON
AMSTERDAM • PARIS • SYDNEY • HAMBURG
STOCKHOLM • ATHENS • TOKYO • MILAN

To Bobby, my technical advisor, with great appreciation

Published November 1991

ISBN 0-373-25470-9

AN IMPERFECT HERO

1

IF THERE HAD BEEN any other way, she would have taken it. Anything would have been more appealing than canceling the celebration they had planned.

Hank was not going to be pleased, either. Not at all. Susan Metcalf let her hand hover above the phone as she searched desperately for some option left unexplored. She found none.

Wondering briefly why she had ever wanted a career in journalism in the first place, she picked up the receiver and punched the numbers that would connect her with the man eagerly waiting for a wife that would not be showing up.

"What do you mean, you aren't coming home?" Hank bellowed, seconds later. "What is it this time?"

"I'm sorry, hon. Tommy's too sick to drive his route. I'm going to have to make his deliveries myself."

The unmistakable sound of a booted foot stomping a hardwood floor echoed across the line. "But that will take you all night!" he raged. "What about our plans?"

"Hank, I'm just as upset as you are, if not more." Susan tried to reason with him. "Playing delivery boy isn't exactly my idea of a birthday party, you know."

"So why don't you order someone else to do it? You're the boss, remember? That's what employees are for."

"Because they are employees, not slaves," the newspaper publisher reminded him. "Most of them already have routes to deliver and the ones that don't, have other obligations."

"You have other obligations, too," Hank argued. "Like a husband who can't remember the last time he made love to his wife."

"It was just last—" Susan stopped abruptly. Damn it, she couldn't remember, either. "Never mind," she said. "The kids won't be back until Sunday. We'll still have the rest of the weekend to ourselves."

"Sure, we will. At least until some urgent story breaks."

"That's not fair, Hank. We've had just as many plans ruined by emergencies at the Seed & Supplies."

"Not since you took over the paper. My work has never been this bad. Hell, Susan, it seems like we never get to spend a whole night in bed together anymore."

Susan didn't have a swift comeback this time. Her husband was right. Tonight was just one of many in the past two years that she hadn't made it home in time to tuck herself in with him.

The newspaper business had always had a natural inclination to flout work schedules and reasonable hours. Her becoming the publisher and editor-in-chief of the tricounty biweekly two years ago had only made the situation worse.

Deliberately softening her voice, Susan repeated her old, worn-out defense: "You knew it was going to be like this when we talked about buying the *Gazette*. You said you understood. You said you would support me."

"I didn't know it was going to be this bad," Hank said wearily. "Damn it, Suz, I never even get to see you."

Susan swallowed hard and gave the tears clinging to her lashes a quick swipe. Too late, she realized her ink-stained fingers would leave traces of black that would mingle with the salty drops and streak across her cheeks like cheap mascara.

"It'll get better, Hank. I promise it's going to get better. The *Gazette* is just now pulling out of the red. A few months more and I'll be able to hire some extra help. It'll get better then. I promise."

"Yeah, right." Hank didn't bother to hide his skepticism. "In the meantime, there goes our weekend alone."

"I'm sorry," Susan apologized yet again. "But it's my paper. It's my responsibility."

"Well, it's going to be grounds for divorce if you don't learn to delegate."

Susan caught her breath. "I know you didn't mean that, so I'm going to pretend you didn't even say it." Nothing but silence followed her brave words and she hurried on to fill the void. "Look, I can't argue with you about it anymore. The sooner I hit the road, the sooner I'll be home."

"Suz, wait!" Hank hastened to make amends. "Why don't you let me take half the deliveries for you. Maybe then we'll get done in time to go to bed together."

Susan was already shaking her head at her end of the line. "I only have one tape recording of the route."

"Well, then, I'll drive and you can throw," he offered desperately. "At least we'll be together."

"Hank, I appreciate the offer but it won't work. The car can barely hold me and the newspapers. There's no room for you." She hurriedly tagged on another apology to soften her rejection. "I'm sorry. I'll get done as quick as I can."

"Right," he answered. "I guess you really don't need me—for anything."

"Hank, that's not—"

He hung up before she could finish. Frustrated and not knowing what to do about it, Hank rubbed his hand across the scalp that suddenly seemed too small to contain the sizzling-hot temper brewing inside. Damn it! Marriage wasn't supposed to be like this.

The tapered candles adorning the table he had set for two snapped like matchsticks between his fingers. The colorful bouquet of flowers he had bought took a high dive, then went sailing toward the wall as a recently polished boot kicked it out of his path.

Hank slammed his way out the front door and swore steadily as he made the fifteen-minute drive across town to the small joint that passed for a nightclub in Morristown, Arkansas, population 7,826.

The first shot of whiskey slid down to his belly and sent ripples up his spine. Truth be told, he hated the taste of the amber liquid and usually opted for the mellower effects of a pitcher of beer. But Hank wasn't feeling very mellow tonight.

He set the empty glass back on the bar and aimed it toward Beau, the bartender, for another round even as he told himself that drinking wasn't the answer. Unfortunately, he didn't know what the answer was or even if there was one.

He was losing her. And he knew it. Sometimes it seemed that he had been losing a little bit of Susan every moment since the day he had first made her his. Sometimes he was afraid that she had actually never been his at all, and he feared that at any moment Susan would realize that herself.

Only two things had enabled him to keep her this long: financial dependence and physical need. But Hank knew that the *Gazette* was becoming more financially secure with each issue. And as for sex... Well, okay, so he'd lied. He *could* remember the last time. But obviously Susan couldn't. That seemed a pretty fair indication of his desirability as far as his wife was concerned.

Hank continued to brood as he raised the refill to his mouth. The only thing he felt sure about these days was the fact that his marriage couldn't go on as it was much longer. Lifting a glass at least gave him something to do until he did figure out his problems, and Hank knew he needed the illusion that he was doing something.

He was just recovering from his second shot of the fiery alcohol when a feminine form arranged itself on the stool beside him and requested, "A vodka martini, dry," in a breathy low-pitched voice.

Uneasy at the exotic creature's proximity, Hank tried to discreetly pull back a few inches. A slender hand adorned with painted nails reached out to halt his retreat.

"You know, it really isn't fair, Hank," Sandra Kellogg purred in his ear. "You seem to be getting better while the rest of us just get older."

Hank felt a flush rise to his face and awkwardly tried another side step. His predator pressed closer, trapping him between her soft, voluptuous body and the solid mahogany bar. A musky-scented cloak closed around him and the whiskey began to blaze like wildfire through his veins.

"I hope Susan appreciates what she has," the woman practically mewed. "You certainly wouldn't be here alone if you were mine."

Hank's broad shoulders slumped and the heat inside began to simmer. "Susan doesn't care."

The blonde smiled sympathetically and her hand began to knead the muscles of the strong arm braced against the bar. She could feel his strength and knew that her words had not been mere flattery; Hank Metcalf had definitely improved with age.

Sandra softened her moves toward the big man, approaching him as cautiously as a hunter would a wild animal caught in a trap and still hurting.

Hank never stood a chance.

IT WAS A HELL of a way to spend her thirtieth birthday, Susan decided.

Alone. Driving a car that was running only on dreams and prayers through a deserted rural stretch of highway at three o'clock in the morning.

Alone. Traveling through a pitch dark that was broken far too infrequently by a brief glimpse of the moon, as it dashed from one cloud to the next.

A light drizzle dampened the windshield, adding yet another layer of darkness to the blacktop road. A tape recorder, her sole companion, occupied the passenger seat, squeaking and squelching as it advanced the tape inside the cassette. With the index finger of her right hand she stabbed Rewind and then hit Stop and Play in quick succession.

"The next drop-off is a mile and a half from the Petersons'. You'll pass a grain silo on your left...." Check. "Then you go over a narrow wooden bridge...." Check. "On the other side of the creek, you'll come to a—"

"Damn it!" Gripping the steering wheel with both hands, Susan struggled to keep control as a sharp S curve suddenly loomed before her headlights. The rear wheels slipped ominously but she held her vintage Volkswagen Beetle on the road, shifting swiftly into low gear to slow it down.

"The next drop will be . . ."

"Oh, shut up!" She punched Stop using more force than was necessary and treated herself to a moment of glorious silence before pressing the now familiar sequence of buttons again. Rewind. Stop. Play.

". . . come to a sharp curve, better slow down . . ."

"Thanks for the warning," she scoffed.

The tape ignored her. "Then about another half a mile down the road you'll come to a stand of trees. Actually there's two stands of trees. Mrs. Kellogg's driveway is right between . . ."

"Shoot!" Ignoring the grinding of the gears, Susan quickly shifted down, her foot furiously pumping the brake pedal. When the valiant Don Quixote, as the car was affectionately known, still refused to halt, she jerked up on the hand brake and brought the '71 Volkswagen Beetle to a violent stop fifty yards past the driveway.

Still swearing profusely, she rammed the stick into reverse. The Don obediently backed up in short, spine-jarring hops, then shuddered to death at the edge of the gravel entrance.

Susan took a deep breath, mentally counting backward from one hundred by fives—she found it far more effective than simply counting to ten. Then she took a very deep breath and reached behind her for one of the rolled-up newspapers that had filled the back seat.

Her hand fumbled for a moment, searching for a paper to throw. Unfortunately, the remaining few had somehow scattered themselves into every nook and cranny of the small interior. Thank goodness she only had about fifty of the three hundred papers left to deliver. Not that there was much point in hurrying now.

Susan grimaced at that thought. It didn't take her writer's imagination to guess that Hank would have nursed his temper with a pitcher of beer at the Jubilee. It seemed to have become his standard procedure during the past year or so. She wasn't particularly fond of the habit, but Hank had taken over most of the household and parental responsibilities since she had bought out the paper and Susan knew it would be foolish to begrudge him a few drinks with the boys now and then.

Besides, she thought, nagging him about it was only going to give her husband one more thing to complain about. She sighed as she finally located the pack of renegade scrolls huddled on the floor behind the passenger seat. Even if she was able to get home at a decent hour, her husband wasn't likely to be in any shape to take advantage of her.

"Damn it, it's not supposed to be like this," she protested to the dark clouds overhead. "I had it all planned, and this definitely is not the way my thirties were supposed to begin."

This was supposed to be *her* decade. Within the next ten years the paper would be entrenched in the black. Her children would be out of college and beginning careers, maybe even families, of their own. At long last, she and her husband would have the luxury of time and money to spend on nothing and no one but each other.

She had it all planned, by golly, and she wasn't about to let anything screw it up, especially not a lousy beginning. Shoot, she had never much cared for birthdays, anyway.

Clenching her fist around one tightly rolled copy of the *Gazette*, Susan brought her arm up and around, staring at the Saturday Shopper's edition with a determined expression her family would have recognized instantly.

One more year and she would be able to replace all the antiquated printing equipment that was constantly contributing to her difficulties. By next summer, she might even be able to take on another full-time staff member. And pretty soon her son, Jake, would be old enough to work part-time, if his interest in journalism held through puberty.

"Hank is just going to have to learn a little patience, that's all," she mumbled out loud. "It's all going to be worth the wait someday." If she didn't believe that with all her heart, Susan would never have sacrificed the time she might have spent with her family. Sure, her career was important to her, but that didn't mean she intended Hank and the kids to take a back seat to the newspaper forever.

She would prove that to Hank by making up to him for this latest disappointment. Kim and Jake wouldn't return from the Methodist church's back-to-school youth retreat until Sunday afternoon. She and Hank would still have all day tomorrow to themselves—and tomorrow night.

The next edition of the *Gazette* wasn't due out until Wednesday. She could afford to give herself a day off from the paper. Then she could devote Saturday strictly to Hank and remind him just how sexy a thirty-year-old career woman could be.

Susan stretched her arm out the open window and pitched the newspaper in a smooth, clean arc toward the far end of the drive. The anger over having to play delivery boy was forgotten for a moment as she admired her throw. Young Tommy Slocum, the regular on the route, couldn't have done it better. As a relief pitcher, she admitted, she wasn't half bad.

"Yes, sir," Susan concluded decisively. "I'll make it up to Hank and he'll see. It's all going to be worth it in the long run."

She had been so caught up in her pep talk, Susan didn't even see the man exiting the divorcée's house until the slam of the front door snared her attention. Quickly she twisted the key in the ignition, offering urgently whispered words of encouragement to the car to start on the first try just this once.

The old campaigner gave it a valiant effort, making all the appropriate noises but failing to make the catch. Glancing down the drive, Susan kept trying the starter, hoping anxiously that whoever saw the old Volkswagen would assume that young Tommy was driving, as usual. Her press credentials would be worthless if her readership believed their newspaper publisher was spying on them in the wee hours of the morning.

Of course, the moon chose that instant to reinitiate its peek-a-boo game. As innocent as a baby playing with an old cloth diaper, the bright yellow orb popped out from behind a cloud, cheerfully announcing "I see you!" to the world at large.

In that moment Susan saw her world clearly, too, and she forgot all about the Don's faulty starter. As if she were scrunched in a theater seat with eyes glued to the big screen, she watched the man stoop to pick up the magnificently thrown paper before straightening slowly to face her square on.

She knew that face. Knew it intimately. The close-cut black hair. The wide brow sliced through with a thin, slanting scar. The bottomless dark eyes. Susan knew that face as well as her own, probably even better. She had never cared much for her own reflection, but she could have looked at that masculine face for hours on end. In fact, she often had done just that, and now her mind easily filled in the shadows the moonlight couldn't reach.

By its own will, her hand turned the key again and this time Don Quixote caught the spark. The car began to ease forward, as if being pulled on a string by the moonbeam.

Susan never would be able to recall the drive home. Tomorrow, fifty angry customers would call demanding to know what had happened to their papers, but she would forget all about them for now.

When she pulled into her own driveway a half hour later, Susan moved like an automaton. Her mind was numb, her body in shock and her eyes still wide with disbelief. Only her mental reflexes kept her going, the drill sergeant in the left quadrant of her brain taking charge in the moment of crisis. Turn off the car, it ordered. Set the brake. Open the door. March. Left, right, left, right. Into the house, up the stairs.

Only when she'd reached their bedroom, when she stared down at their empty bed with its covers still stretched taut across the mattress, did Susan finally let herself believe what she had seen.

Hank. Her Hank. The man she had been happily married to for over thirteen years. The man she could have sworn would never cheat on her. The man leaving Sandra Kellogg's house at three in the morning, his shirttails flapping loosely, his buttons still half undone. Her husband. The rotten bastard!

She wanted to kill him. And her, that other woman. That slut, Sandra Kellogg.

She couldn't, of course. And it wouldn't change what had happened except that she'd be enjoying her revenge on death row. So she'd just have to get rid of him another way. Fetching the lawn-size garbage bags from under the kitchen sink, Susan systematically began to empty his drawers and strip his closet, stuffing a huge green plastic sack full with Hank's things.

She paused briefly when the squeal of tires turning sharply into the drive announced her husband's return. Seconds later, the sound of booted feet pounding up the stairs spurred her hands to stuff the bag even faster.

Hank came to an abrupt halt in the doorway of their bedroom. "Susan?" Her name came out as a plea. "Susan, stop. Listen to me."

"Listen to what?" she asked. Her hands swiftly twisted a tie around the full bag, then yanked another sack from the box. "Excuses? Explanations? Go ahead. I can't wait to hear them."

But Hank suddenly seemed at a total loss for words.

"Come on, Hank. It can't be that hard. There are plenty of clichés to cover the situation. 'Appearances are deceiving.' 'It wasn't what it looked like.' Go ahead," she encouraged him recklessly.

But he just stared at her like a man turned to stone.

"Come on, Hank, tell me," she urged again, whirling around to meet him face-to-face. "Tell me you just ran into Sandra at the Jube. Tell me she had car trouble and you offered her a ride home. Tell me she invited you in for coffee just to say thanks."

She dropped the clothes she was about to jam into the sack and took a step closer to him, flicking one of his unsecured buttons with the tip of her finger. "Tell me her sink stopped up or her commode overflowed and that's why you had to take off your shirt. Tell me she was just so damned grateful she had to kiss you and that's why you have her lipstick all over your face. That that's why you reek of her perfume. Tell me, Hank."

Susan took another step toward him, narrowing the gap between them to mere inches. Her slender hands grasped his shoulders, her nails sank into the heavy muscles and she shook him. At least she tried to. "Tell me that's what happened, Hank. Tell me what I'm thinking is wrong. Tell me you didn't make love to that woman."

"I, I . . ." he stammered helplessly, then swallowed hard.

"Tell me, Hank!" she insisted again, almost hysterically.

Hank bowed his head, shaking it slowly. Stepping back from his wife's digging nails, he reached around her to grasp the trash bags she had filled. Slinging the closed one over his shoulder, he gathered the opening of the other in the opposite hand and turned to leave.

Susan clutched at his arm as he reached the top of the stairs, pleading with him. "Hank! Tell me I'm wrong. Tell me nothing happened!"

Hank shrugged her aside and began walking down the stairs.

She watched him until he reached the landing, but he never looked back. He kept heading straight for the front door.

"Hank!" Too late, Susan tore down the stairs after him, reaching the door just in time to watch his red Chevy screech out of the drive. "You come back here! I'm not through with you yet!"

The pickup was already turning the corner. A moment later, its red taillights vanished from sight. *He probably can't wait to get back to his mistress,* Susan thought bitterly. Bastard. Slut. They deserved each other.

"Go ahead!" she yelled after him. "Go back to her. See if I care!"

She slammed the door shut and let herself collapse on the living-room sofa. She drew her knees up to support her chin and planted her feet on the cushions—just as she had asked her children a hundred times not to sit.

I don't care, Susan told herself. *I won't care. No two-timing husband is worth caring about.* She repeated this litany again and again. Quietly at first, then getting louder with each repetition as if volume were somehow an indication of truth. "I don't care. I don't care. He isn't worth it."

When the chant became a high-pitched scream, Susan's thin structure of self-preservation cracked. The tears began to spill slowly, gathering strength with each drop, forcing the crack to grow wider until it burst open with gut-wrenching wails of anguish that pierced the darkness.

HANK HEARD ONLY SILENCE as he drove through the midnight blue that stretches between a setting moon and a rising sun. Fond memories guided him east, and when dawn came looking, it found him sitting on a levee overlooking the drought-stricken Mississippi.

The record-low water level revealed scars on the banks that had been hidden from eyes for hundreds of years. Sandbars lay stripped naked, their ends curling toward each other as if they were ashamed of their nudity and longed for the protective cover of muddy waters.

Hank sat beside the ailing "Old Man," sharing the river's pain, commiserating with his dearest friend. He, too, felt exposed. The pretense that his marriage was all right had evaporated in the face of his growing anger, just as the mighty Mississippi's depth had been stolen away by the past summer's unrelenting heat wave.

"Everything has to end sometime," he consoled the river. "Even droughts and bad marriages."

The light drizzle that had teased the parched soil all night heard him and took pity, giving in at last to the full promise of rain and giving proof to Hank's words.

The earth and river sighed with relief and the rich scent of soil greeting rain filled the air. Hank drank in the smell as he stood to leave the levee, his clothes already drenched by the sudden downpour. He let out a sigh of his own and felt a weight lift from his shoulders.

It was over. The pretense, the bottled-up anger, the resentment were all being released like rain from the dark, heavy clouds. The silent suffering had come to an end. But his brief satisfaction fled as another thought took hold. It was over. His marriage, his home, his life with Susan had all been lost.

It was a hell of a price to pay for relief.

2

THE WATER SLOWED to a steady drip but refused to cease altogether. Susan swore at the leaky shower head and vowed to replace it with a new, improved model if it didn't straighten out its act. The threat did the trick and the last drop slid meekly down the drain.

She stepped out of the tub and purposely chose the coarsest towel to dry off with. The friction was a relief after the complete numbness that had claimed her in the hours since Hank's departure.

Susan had finally summoned the strength to pull herself off the sofa, hoping it all had been a terrible dream. However, the cold bed sheets, empty drawers and barren closet in the master bedroom had all given testimony to Hank's absence.

It had really happened. She had caught Hank leaving the scene herself. It would have been impossible to turn a blind eye even if she had been the sort of woman who could tolerate that kind of behavior—which Susan wasn't.

She fumbled for her glasses, then cleared the fog off the bathroom mirror. Puffy, pink-rimmed eyes stared back at her through quarter-inch-thick spectacles, the left eye wandering slightly more than usual.

"It's a good thing she's smart because she'll never be homecoming queen."

Susan could hear the remark as clearly as if the optometrist who'd made it were standing in the room right next to her. He wasn't, of course. The echo of his words just clung to her mind the way carelessly cruel remarks have a tendency to do. Not that it had been meant cruelly. It was just a fact that little girls with pop-bottle-lensed glasses and a lazy eye seldom grew up to win beauty pageants.

In all honesty, it was a fact that had never bothered her much. After all, she had been compensated in brains for far more than she had lacked in looks. The resulting package had been good enough for Hank when she was fifteen. She didn't see why it shouldn't suffice at thirty. Obviously her husband thought differently.

Susan took a step back and studied her mirror image again. Against her better judgment, she began making comparisons to the still-trim, still-beautiful ex-cheerleader. She had never been in the same league as Sandra Kellogg. In truth, she had never cared to be. Appearances had never really seemed that important to her.

Besides, if anything, Susan knew that she had improved with age. The sharp angles of her face hadn't set well on a child but they wore her thirty years with grace. Actually, she didn't look that much different now than she had at fifteen. The only real difference was that now her age and her face were more suited to each other. And, she no longer had to worry about pimples.

Bearing two children had added a few stretch marks and a few pounds creating a few curves. Unfortunately, her breasts had refused to retain the temporary state of fullness brought on by pregnancy and nursing. But Hank hadn't seemed to mind that. He had always said that any more than a mouthful was a waste.

Susan found herself smiling as she recalled the softly teasing, often repeated comment. The smile slipped as suddenly as it had appeared, falling into a wry frown. So why hadn't her husband had an affair with a flat-chested bimbo instead of one of the well-endowed variety? Or didn't bimbos come in more than one style?

"Damn him!" she cursed again. "How could he do this to us? Why did he have to ruin everything?"

Her reflection had no answers to offer and Susan turned away from it. Only one person had the answers and he wasn't talking, blast him.

She swept an arm across the vanity and rid herself of Hank's remainders with one fell swoop. His old-fashioned straight-edged razor, the red toothbrush and a black plastic wide-toothed comb crashed against the bottom of the metal wastebasket.

Thirteen years trashed in a single night. Susan shook her head in disgust. Everything they had worked for tossed out like yesterday's garbage. All for the sake of a roll in the hay with the thrice-married, thrice-divorced, try-try-again Sandra Kellogg.

"Where the heck was the man's mind while his body was screwing up our lives?" Susan spoke out loud, wincing as her ears caught the bitter pun.

She went back into their bedroom to scrounge up clean clothes but was sidetracked by the framed pictures adorning the dresser. Shot after shot revealed the brief history of her two children. Baby pictures, poses with Santa, preschool graduations, Little League uniforms. All so innocent, so unsuspecting.

How could Hank do this to them? Whatever doubts she had about their relationship, she knew he loved those kids. How could he destroy their home like this?

How was she going to explain his behavior to her children when she didn't understand it herself?

"Where's Daddy? Oh, probably at his girlfriend's house. They're having a sleep-over." No, definitely not like that. She sighed. Thank goodness the children wouldn't be home till tomorrow. Maybe by then she would have come up with some reasonable explanation, some means of breaking it to them gently.

Susan felt the sting of fresh tears and quickly pressed her fingers against closed eyelids to hold back the flood. There had already been more than enough of that.

A resounding crash of thunder underscored that thought and she jumped as the boomer echoed in the distance. Dashing to her bedroom window, she yanked back the curtains and stared out at the pouring rain.

Rain. Real rain, not a mere mist. Sweet, blessed rain. Scrambling into a pair of jeans, an ink-stained sweatshirt and her favorite worn-out sneakers as she went, Susan stumbled down the stairs and flung open the front door to verify the fact. It was true. It really was raining. The drought was over and the timing couldn't have been better.

"Forget Hank," she ordered herself sternly. "Forget Sandra. You've got a newspaper to print, woman, and the best news of the decade is falling right on your doorstep."

She grabbed the phone and dialed her photographer, David Sinclair. "Get pictures," she instructed him. "Lots of pictures. Shoot tractors stuck in mud and raindrops on withered crops. Get people with umbrellas and children with galoshes and farmers with tears in their eyes. We'll do a photo page to celebrate. And hurry up in case it decides to stop. Call me at the office if you have any questions."

Susan hung up without waiting for David's confirmation, already feeling better. If anything could take her mind off her crumbling marriage, it would be the *Gazette*. And if that strategy didn't succeed, she decided as she drove the Don through the wet streets, at least she would be doing something more constructive than crying her eyes out at home.

ON THE OTHER SIDE of town, the downpour was belting out a rousing tune on the tin roof of the Farmer's Seed & Supplies. Inside the barnlike structure, an accompaniment of farmers and gardeners joined the refrain.

"It's about damned time!"

"Careful, there. We don't want to press our luck."

"That's right. Hallelujah, I say."

Whether they were growing three hundred acres of rice or a patch of peppers and tomatoes in the backyard, the consensus was the same.

"He sure took his time about it."

"Watch it, He could still change his mind."

"That's right. Hallelujah, I say. Think rain!"

Hank let the joyous conversations flow around him. No one seemed to notice that he talked even less than usual—not that he could have added much to the continuously repeated lyrics.

Neither of his partners thought to ask why he was there after he had made such a big deal about having Saturday off. Heck, it seemed half the citizens of Morristown had come to the store to join the spontaneous celebration. It would have been more curious if he hadn't shown up.

Despite the unending tide of visitors sweeping in throughout the day, Hank found himself with very little to do. Even his best customers were too excited to think about fertilizers or farming equipment. They just hung around, blending into the sea of happy, smiling faces.

"Guess we know what Susan's next headline's going to be, don't we, Metcalf?" Junior Brown finally shouted above the other voices.

One corner of Hank's tightly compressed mouth quirked in response. For once, he doubted that Susan's mind was occupied by the story of the hour. The vision of her livid face glaring furiously at him returned to his mind, and hope flickered briefly. Perhaps he had underestimated the depth of her feelings.

But no, he told himself. Susan might have been shocked by his alleged behavior, but she hadn't been destroyed. She was the strongest woman he knew. Hank was sure it wouldn't take her long to recognize the fact that she was better off without him—if she hadn't realized it already.

"There's no room for you," Susan had told him last night. Her husband was all too aware that the words applied to more than the limited amount of space inside the '71 Beetle used to make the rural-route deliveries. The growing success of the newspaper and the growing independence of his children were proof that he was being squeezed out of his family faster than eleven-year-old Jake's toes poked holes in a brand-new pair of sneakers.

Something wet splashed onto his cheek and Hank looked up instantly to spot the leak in the roof. But it wasn't a drop of rain that had hit him. The bead of moisture slid farther down, leaving a trace of salt on his lips; he hurriedly brushed a sleeve across his face to erase the evidence.

Hank's eyes scanned the boisterous crowd for potential witnesses. Fortunately, no one seemed to have noticed his moment of weakness and he quickly retreated to the privacy of a storeroom, waving an inventory sheet at anyone who questioned his departure.

"That's Metcalf for you," he heard Joe Camden, one of his partners say. "A real workhorse. Neither drought nor flood nor celebration shall keep him from his appointed duties."

"Yeah, right," Hank jeered behind closed doors. "A workhorse who had the stupidity to get himself hitched to a thoroughbred." He knew he was a hard worker, a steady and reliable provider for his family, but Metcalf didn't kid himself. He had neither the ambition nor the ability to keep up with Susan. He had always known it was only a matter of time before he got left behind in her dust.

Truth be told, he had been darned lucky ever to have been given the chance to travel even partway through life with the woman he loved.

He hadn't needed Susan's friends and family to point out the fact that his high school sweetheart had him outclassed in every subject. It had been obvious to everyone that the honor student could have done much better than a boy whose greatest achievement had been getting her pregnant. That one feat had secured him at least a temporary place beside Susan, and Hank had never regretted it.

Tugging his wallet out of his back pocket, Hank flipped through his collection of school pictures with unabashed pride. Maybe he hadn't accomplished much else, he thought, but nobody could fault his ability to sire great kids. Kim and Jake were the best any father could hope for.

"Hey, Hank. Come on." Joe poked his head through the door. "We're going to close up early in honor of the weather. The Jube's giving drinks on the house to the first hundred soaking-wet customers."

"Yeah, sure. Be right there," Hank said. He gave the kids' photos one last look, then slipped the wallet back in his pocket. Maybe a drink was just what he needed to ease the sudden tightness in his throat.

He joined the rowdy crowd flowing out the S&S doors and let it carry him down the street to the club, where a full-fledged party was under way.

As Hank snagged a stool at the far end of the long bar and pulled himself out of the babbling stream of people, he couldn't help but remember the days when he would have fought through the mob and hurried home for a family dinner. *Those days are gone*, he reminded himself. *Long gone*. Once more, he found himself with nothing to do besides lift a glass.

He had his complimentary beer raised halfway to his mouth when he looked past the rim and spotted Sandra Kellogg coming through the club's front door. His glass hit the bar so hard, the brew slopped over the sides. He tried to duck behind Buddy Owen's broad figure, but it was no use. Sandra spotted him immediately and began to zero in on him without hesitation.

Instinct told Hank to run for his life and he beat a hasty path to the Jube's rear exit, ignoring the call of Sandra's voice. He didn't slow down until he was safely on the road and out of the maneater's hungry reach. He was halfway home before he even realized where he was going.

He stopped for a red light two blocks from the house and thought it over. Should he go home? Was there any point? Susan probably wouldn't even let him in the front door. But maybe if he talked to her, maybe if he told her everything that had happened, maybe . . .

Maybe what? Hank asked himself. *Maybe she'll let you stick around a little longer. Is that really what you want, Metcalf? Just to hang around until she forces you to leave?*

He sat through two green lights before an angry toot behind him made him jar his foot on the gas pedal. "Old Red" headed for the familiar carport just as surely as a horse finds his way back to the barn at feeding time. Hank pulled the truck up short at the edge of the driveway.

The house was dark. There was no sign of life. For one frightful moment, Hank feared that Susan had taken the kids and left. Then reason took hold and reasserted itself in his muddled brain.

All of Susan's friends and most of her family lived in Morristown. Hell, the newspaper was here. Where else was the woman going to go?

Hank's powers of rationalization continued to improve until they slowly began to reach their normal functioning state. The kids were still at their church youth retreat. That's why it was so quiet. But where was Susan? Neither the station wagon nor the old Bug were in sight.

Panic tugged again at his nerve endings until the obvious answer asserted itself. The newspaper, of course. Where else would she be? He had obviously overestimated his importance when he had thought that for once the front page wouldn't come before their marriage.

"That's just great," Hank muttered. "Our future is on the rocks and she's at the damned *Gazette!*"

His temper surged to new heights as he made the short trip from the house to the paper's office a few blocks away. If anyone had seen his face as he stormed into the building, they would have dialed 911 to report that a murder was about to take place.

Susan considered doing just that when she looked up from the layout table to see who was disturbing her attempts at concentration. However, it wasn't her life that she was concerned about. The calm, even-tempered woman who was known for keeping cool in the face of her husband's volcanic outbursts had discovered a very interesting fact in the past sixteen hours: Hank's temper had nothing on hers.

"I figured I'd find you here," her husband said. "This comes before everything else, doesn't it? Hell, I don't even know why I bothered to come."

"Well, that makes two of us, then," Susan told him. "I can't believe you even have the nerve to face me after last night."

"Last night's precisely why I did come looking for you," Hank said. "I thought we should discuss it. I thought we should try to fix things before they got any worse, but I guess I'm already too late. If all you can think about is the next issue when our marriage is falling apart, then I suppose there's really nothing left to discuss."

Susan turned her back on him and pretended to focus on the dummy she had been laying out. "What did you expect when you walked out without a word? Did you think I would just sit home weeping and wringing my hands until you came back?"

That was precisely what Hank had wanted to think, but he wasn't about to admit it. Instead, he just kept up his stone-wall facade and refused to answer.

After thirteen years, however, Susan had learned to read his silences quite well. She glanced at him casually over her shoulder. "That is what you wanted, isn't it, Hank? Well, I'm sorry to have disappointed you. But a man who can't be faithful isn't worth that many tears."

Hank shook his head in disbelief. "You don't even care, do you?" His left boot pawed the floor as if he were a bull preparing to charge at any second. "You don't give a damn if I do sleep with someone else!"

His wife spun around in a fury. "Oh, I give a damn, Hank! In fact I've done nothing but damn your soul ever since I saw you leaving Sandra's house!" Susan choked at the mention of the other woman's name. A sob managed to escape before she could bring herself back under control. "How could you go to her, Hank? How could you?"

Her husband straightened his spine, squared his shoulders and prepared to stand his ground. "Well, what did you expect me to do, Suz? How long did you really think I was going to settle for being last on your list of priorities?"

"I never put you last," Susan protested angrily. "Damn it, Hank. Everything I do for the *Gazette* is for us. You, Kim, Jake—all of us. We have so much invested in it, I can't afford not to make it work. Couldn't you understand that? Couldn't you just have been patient a little longer?"

"Patient for how long?" Hank demanded. "Until you've doubled circulation? Until the *Gazette* is a daily with statewide distribution? How long was I supposed to wait, Susan?" His large hands clamped around her shoulders and shook her briefly. "Damn it, I needed you last night! Not next year or the year after that!"

She shoved him away, her own fists clenched in anger. "And since I wasn't there you decided to take Sandra instead. Is that right?" Tears welled in her eyes and began to spill down her face unchecked. "Is that why you went home with her? You were horny and any warm body would do? How many other times has she taken my place?"

"No, it wasn't like that!" Hank shouted back. "Nobody has ever taken your place. Not Sandra, not anybody. They couldn't."

He wanted to touch her, to hold her, but he didn't dare. "Damn it, Susan. I wanted you. Why couldn't you have just come home?"

"Don't you think I wanted to?" Susan stared at him incredulously. "For crying out loud, Hank. It was my birthday! Do you really think I preferred spending it with three hundred newspapers instead of you?"

"Then why didn't you come home?" he asked again.

"Because what I preferred didn't matter," she said. "The blasted papers had to be delivered and I had to do it."

"Yeah, yeah. The same old song-and-dance routine. All you're really saying is that your precious paper comes first and I come last."

"No!" Susan buried her face in her hands and desperately tried to hold on to her sanity. *Damn it, he was the one who should be on trial here. Not her.*

She flung her hands down and glared at her husband. "I'm not going to let you make me the villain, Hank. You're the one that cheated last night."

Hank turned away from her and studied the framed award-winning front pages hanging on the office walls. Silence stretched across the room for several seconds before he finally broke it with a husky whisper.

"What if—" he paused to clear his throat, then tried again "—what if I told you nothing happened? Would you believe me?"

"You're a little late with that, aren't you?" Susan laughed bitterly and shook her head again. "Shoot, Hank, I practically handed you an alibi last night. All you had to do was say 'Yes, Susan. That's what happened.' Maybe I could have let myself believe it then. But not now. You can't really expect me to believe a tale like that after you walked out on me."

Hank swore beneath his breath, then turned to stare at her through glistening black eyes. "Then where do we go from here? Do you want me to move out?"

"I thought you had."

"Well, you had already stuffed all my things in trash bags like yesterday's garbage." Hank felt another surge of anger as he thought of the plastic sacks still sitting in the back of his truck. "Hell, Susan. Couldn't you have at least put everything in a suitcase?"

"We don't have any," Susan reminded him. "We've never gone anywhere to need them."

"Then you could at least have used a box or something. Do you know how it made me feel, hauling off everything in garbage bags?"

Susan shrugged her shoulders. "It seemed appropriate at the time."

Hank sighed. He obviously wasn't going to get any sympathy from his wife today. "I guess I'll just check into the motel for now."

"Motel? I thought . . ."

"What?"

"Nothing," Susan answered too quickly. "Never mind." She licked her lips nervously and hurried on to the next pressing problem. "What about the kids? What do we tell Kim and Jake?"

Hank rubbed his hand across his forehead, his thumb and forefinger pressing against his temples, trying to relieve the unrelenting pressure building there. "I don't know. It isn't necessary to go into details, is it? I'm sure we both want to spare them as much unpleasantness as possible."

"I want what is best for them," Susan stated firmly.

Hank nodded. "At least we agree on one thing." He began to move wearily toward the door. "I'll pick them up at the church and tell them myself, since I'm the one that's leaving."

Susan almost agreed. Then she remembered that according to him, this was all her fault. "No, that's all right. I'll tell them myself."

Hank looked back at her. "Don't you trust me?"

She let her glasses slip down on her nose so she could peer over the top to give him her best I-wasn't-born-yesterday look. "That's rather a stupid question, considering the situation now, isn't it?"

A crimson tide made its way up Hank's neck and flushed his face. "All right," he gave in quickly. "We'll tell them together. I'll pick you up tomorrow. Two o'clock. At the house. We'll go meet the church van together."

"Fine."

"And Susan," he warned just a second before the door closed behind him, "this time, don't keep me waiting."

3

"NOW, REMEMBER," Susan instructed her husband again, "we're not going to say anything until we get home."

"I remember," Hank growled back, earning another glare from his wife.

Neither of them had counted on the church van being an hour late. The two of them had spent the past sixty minutes leaning against Hank's truck, doing their best to antagonize each other without attracting the attention of the other parents standing nearby.

"And no arguing in front of them," she added. "Just stick to the facts we agreed on."

"Susan, you don't have to keep reminding me. I don't want to make this any harder on them than you do."

"I just don't want there to be any confusion."

"There's not."

"Fine." She clamped her lips back together and began folding and unfolding her arms as if she couldn't figure out exactly where they were supposed to go.

Hank transferred his weight to his right foot and sighed.

"Do you have to keep doing that?" his wife asked. "You sound like an old tire with a slow leak."

He shifted his eyes toward her without turning his head and deliberately sighed again.

Susan thrust out her chin and resumed her plan to ignore him. She managed to count backward from one thousand by fives all the way to nine hundred sixty before she lost track.

"We've just decided to give each other some space for a while." She repeated the story they had decided on. "That's all. There's no need to mention . . . umm, anything more."

"I know. It was my suggestion, remember? After all, there's no reason to alarm them with talk about . . . uhh, something else."

"Fine."

"All right."

Nine hundred ninety-five. Nine hundred ninety. Nine hundred eighty-five. "Oh, hell." Susan surrendered. Counting simply wasn't going to work this time. "Why don't we just say it. They're going to. You know it's the first thing they're going to ask."

"Go ahead," Hank invited. "If that's what you want, just say so."

"I didn't say that's what I wanted, but isn't that what we're headed for?"

"You tell me. You're the one who's supposed to have all the answers."

"Not this time," Susan informed him glumly.

"Well, you'd better come up with them soon. They're here."

Both straightened and moved toward the blue van that was coming to a halt in the church parking lot. The side door slid open and a swarm of teenagers and preteens spilled out, tumbling over each other in a mad scramble for possessions.

The senior Metcalfs put their marital crisis aside for a moment as they searched for their children. Long, sleek, dark Kim was easy to spot as she stood waiting, obviously amused, while three ninth-grade boys jousted for the right to carry the eighth-grader's sleeping bag. The contenders relinquished the contest readily at the appearance of Kim's very large, very formidable father.

Jake was sighted almost as easily. Susan hid the beginnings of a smile behind her hand as the youth finally unfolded his gangly limbs and fell out the door—a young Jimmy Stewart in the making.

Had it not been for the switch in genders, Susan thought for the thousandth time, it would have been easy to believe that she and Hank had merely cloned themselves instead of contributing equally to the makeup of each child.

Kim was definitely her father's daughter, from the sleek black crown of hair and the raven wings lifting above dark fathomless eyes to the strong, supple body that already held the promise of an athletic scholarship. Father and daughter. Twin rivers running deep, etched with strong currents and whirlpools. Swim at your own risk.

And Jake was just as much Susan's son. They shared the same long, loose limbs that would never be grown into, brown eyes gleaming with intellect hidden behind unbelievably thick glasses, and a solid-as-a-rock backbone with the underlying intensity of a quake registering a perfect ten on the Richter scale. Mother and son. Earthshakers locked inside incredibly deceptive landscapes.

Neither parent had deliberately chosen a favorite, Susan assured herself. Like had simply been drawn to like. It was only natural that Kim automatically turned to hug her father first while Jake tripped over his long, narrow feet as he made his way to his mother.

"How was the retreat?"

"Did you have a good time?"

Talk about the retreat got the Metcalfs safely through the drive home and carried them into the house but began to peter out as the kids dumped their bedrolls and duffel bags on the living-room floor.

"Hey, you two know better than that. Take it upstairs where it belongs."

"Aww, Mom!" the juveniles chorused.

Susan pointed her finger toward the second floor. "Now," she ordered. "And hurry up. There's something your father and I need to talk to you about."

"What?" Neither child lifted a finger, choosing to raise the obvious question instead.

"After you take your stuff up. Now, march."

She and Hank ignored their quizzical looks, glancing uncomfortably at each other. Kim and Jake let their curiosity overcome their natural tendency to dawdle over parental requests and hit the stairs at a run.

"Have a seat," Hank told them when they came back down. "And listen carefully, okay? What your mom and I have to say is very important and we don't want there to be any misunderstandings."

"What's wrong?" Kim asked. "Did we do something?"

"No, honey," her mother quickly assured. "Neither you nor Jake are to blame for this. I don't want either of you to think so even for a second."

Their eyes grew big, their faces solemn. "Did somebody die?" Jake asked. "Grandpa Mitchum have another heart attack or—"

"No, son. Everybody's fine," Hank said.

"Then what's wrong?" Kim demanded. "Y'all look so serious. Something has to be wrong."

"Nothing's wrong, exactly. There are just going to be a few changes." Susan had condensed her five-minute prepared speech into one simple sentence; old journalism habits die hard.

"What kind of changes?" Jake cut through to the quick. He hadn't been observing his mother in action for twelve years for nothing.

The departure from their prepared script caused Hank to miss his cue—an error that was swiftly remedied with a sharp jab of Susan's elbow. "Well, mainly that I'm not going to be living here for a while."

"What do you mean?" The children's voices and bodies collided as they both jumped to their feet. "Why not? Where are you going?"

"Now, just sit down. We're going to explain everything in good time." Susan gently pressed her son back down on the couch as Hank did the same with his daughter.

"But . . ."

"Shush now, just listen. Jake. Sit back down, son. All right, now. Just stay calm and listen." Susan took a deep breath and started over again. "Your dad and I have a few problems we need to work out and we thought it would be a good idea if we spent a little time apart to help us clear things up."

"What things?" Jake grabbed the hand his mother extended and clung to it fearfully.

Hank placed a steadying arm around Kim's shoulders. "Just the sort of things that all couples have to deal with. It'll be all right."

Kim swiped a hand across her face, checking the tears that threatened her facade of strength. "But why do you have to leave for y'all to do that?"

"We just thought it would be best, that's all." Susan brushed her daughter's black hair away from her forehead, tucking a strand gently behind the thirteen-year-old's ear.

"Honey, it's going to be all right," her father promised. "I'll be close by. If you need anything, all you have to do is call me."

"No!" Kim pushed her mother's hand away, flinging herself into Hank's arms. "I want to go with you."

"But, pumpkin . . ."

"Honey, no . . ."

Her parents spoke together, equally startled. Susan reached out to pull her daughter back, but recoiled instantly as Kim screamed "No!" again and clung tighter to Hank's solid body.

"I won't stay here! This is all your fault. Daddy's leaving because of you and I want to go with him!"

"No, baby. That's not true." Hank pushed the girl back and tilted her face up, a face that in so many ways reflected his own. "Honey, it's nobody's fault. Your mom and I just need a little time apart."

"No!" Kim buried her nose in his shirt again. "You're leaving because she doesn't have time for us anymore. We don't blame you, Daddy. We hate her, too."

"Kim!" Her father shouted.

"Kim!" Her mother cried.

"Liar!" Her brother accused. "That's not true!" The boy stood bravely to defend and protect his idol. "Take it back, Kim. Take it back, now."

"No. I mean it. She should go away. Not Daddy."

But her father had heard enough of that. He pushed her away from him, forcing her to turn around and face the woman whose heart she had just broken. "Apologize, Kim. Now."

"No."

"Kim!"

"It's all right, Hank. Let her be." Susan put her arms around her loyal son and hugged him tightly. "It's okay, Jake. Kim's entitled to her own feelings. I'm just sorry she didn't tell me about them sooner."

"But she doesn't hate you, Mom! I know she doesn't," Jake insisted.

"I don't think she really does, either. But, sometimes, when you're mad at someone you love, it can feel like you hate them for a little while."

Kim ignored her mother, turning back to Hank, squeezing her arms around his waist. "Please, Daddy. Don't go."

"I have to, honey. But I'm not going far. You and Jake can see me anytime you want to."

"Then let me go with you!"

"Honey, I'm going to be staying at the Carriage Motel. That's no place for you. Now, come on. Straighten up. It's not the end of the world, you know."

"Isn't it?" Kim exclaimed. "I know kids whose parents have split. Half of them haven't even seen their father since the divorce!"

Divorce. The word cut through the air like buckshot, hot and piercing. It ricocheted off the walls and stung their ears repeatedly.

"Nobody said anything about divorce, Kim." Hank started to gently pat her back, then realized how badly his hands were shaking and shoved his fingers into his jeans pockets instead.

"You haven't said it, but isn't that what you're really talking about?"

"No," Susan said. "It's just a separation—"

"That's right," Kim inserted. "A separation. The first stage of divorce."

"Stop saying that word," Jake snapped at her. "You sound like that's what you *want* them to do."

"I don't care," Kim said. "As long as I get to stay with Dad."

"Well, I'm staying with Mom!"

"Guys, stop it." Hank shook his head at them, clucking his tongue. "Look, you're not choosing sides to play ball. Whatever happens, we'll both still be your parents, and you're going to have to accept what we think is best for you. Right now, that means you are both staying here in this house with your mother."

"But, Dad . . ."

"That's enough, Kim. I don't want to hear any more."

His son nodded knowingly. "That's typical."

"Jake!" Susan shook the boy's shoulders.

"Well, it is. Kim says you never have time for us, but you always have time to listen to me. All Dad ever does is yell at everybody. He's always mad for no reason."

"That's a lie," his sister sputtered angrily and would have lunged at her younger brother if their father hadn't held her back.

"Jeez, what's got into you two?" Hank asked. "You sound like you're the ones that need the separation."

"Great, then I'll go with you," Kim agreed readily. "Jake can stay with her."

"You'll go to your room, young lady, Jake will go to his, and you'll both stay put until I say you can come out." Susan met her daughter's defiant stare without flinching. "Now."

Kim looked to her father for support.

"Now," he echoed, crossing his arms over his chest to signify the matter was closed.

The girl stomped up the stairs, then slammed her door with a force that rattled windowpanes throughout the house.

"You too, Jake. Go on up to your room," Hank ordered.

His son started to protest but one look at his mom's no-nonsense expression changed his mind and Jake made his own much quieter exit.

Hank and Susan stared at each other for a moment. "So much for sparing them," Susan muttered. "It seems that they've been more perceptive than we have."

"Yeah." Hank blew out a stream of air and shook his head. "Yeah, I guess they have."

They sank down on opposite ends of the sofa, both lost in their own misery.

Susan stared at the lines on her palm as if there were something written there that she'd never noticed before. "I had no idea Kim resented my work so much," she said after a while. "Why didn't you tell me?"

"Because I didn't know. I thought it was just me that felt that way. Why didn't you tell me about Jake's feelings?"

His wife shook her head in disgust. "Same story. I thought I was the only one you were taking your temper out on."

His jaw clenched angrily. "I haven't been taking out anything on anyone. Lord, you make it sound like I've been beating the lot of you."

"But you know how sensitive Jake is," Susan chastised him. "It would be kinder to beat him than to yell at him."

"I know, I know. You don't have to tell me how to deal with my own son."

"Oh, no? It sounds like we both need someone to tell us about our children. We certainly haven't been reading them right."

Hank stood and began pacing the room slowly, amazed that he could feel so out of place in his own home. He stretched his neck and rubbed the back of his head as if he could dislodge the sense of being lost in vaguely familiar terrain. A little voice began whispering in his ear. *Time to go. Time to go.*

"Do you want me to stick around for a while?" he asked out loud. "In case there's trouble?"

"No." Susan lowered her gaze to her twiddling thumbs. "No, you go on. I think we just all need a little breathing space right now. I'll make sure Kim and Jake know how to reach the motel if they want to talk to you."

Hank nodded and tried to hide his relief by moving slowly toward the front door. He hesitated with one hand on the knob. "Susan?"

"Yes?"

"Is that what you want? A divorce?"

One thumb jabbed the other, its nail scoring a red crescent moon across the opposing knuckle. Susan pressed the injured joint against her mouth, bathing the wound with her tongue. "I'm not sure that we have an alternative anymore."

"Does that mean you're going to file for one?"

"I don't know." She squeezed her eyes tightly and hugged her arms close. "It doesn't have to be decided tonight, though, does it? Can't we talk about that later?"

"Sure." He swung the door back and forth between his palms. "Well, you know where to reach me. Call me if you need anything."

"Fine. Same for you. I mean, if you've forgotten something or, well, whatever."

"Yeah, right."

An awkward silence descended. Their gazes met briefly, uncomfortably, as each pondered the difficulty of saying good-night to a spouse they probably wouldn't be married to much longer.

Finally, Susan simply turned her back on him. *Out of sight, out of—* The door shut quietly behind her. Footsteps faded down the walk. The truck roared to life. Hank left.

Not so difficult, Susan thought.

A foot stomped in the room above. Something solid but nonbreakable hit a wall.

Not so easy. Susan sighed and began to count. *Nine hundred ninety-nine thousand, nine hundred ninety-five.*

4

HANK CRASHED on the queen-size bed, too weary and too cold to bother peeling off his insulated coveralls. He had been living in the padded suit for days; sleeping in it one night wasn't going to make it any filthier or smellier than it was already.

It seemed forever since he had done anything besides sleep and work, with heavy emphasis on the latter. One exhausting day faded into another, one week into the next. The only distinguishing factor was the abrupt change of seasons as the summer drought gave way first to the flash floods and muddy fields caused by autumn downpours and then to the icy silver cloak of an early-winter freeze.

The Farmer's S&S was kept busy throughout. Even a poor harvest was hectic and this year's had scarcely been completed when record low temperatures began holding the delta region of the state hostage.

The busy season and bitter cold temperatures made a mockery of regular working hours. To top things off, Billy Smathers, the regular driver of the propane truck, decided to quit work and go back to college. The S&S could have hired someone to take his place, but with profits down, the partners decided to wait until business picked up in the spring before choosing Billy's replacement. After all, they each had the special license required to drive the fuel truck.

Buddy Owen had carefully worked out a schedule so that the three men would rotate the driving, but after a few days back behind the tanker's wheel, Hank refused to relinquish the driver's seat to either of his partners. When Joe and Buddy had insisted that they share the responsibility, he had claimed that he wanted to do it for nostalgic reasons. Making the propane deliveries had been his first job at the Farmer's Seed & Supplies.

When his partners still argued with him, Hank pointed out that he was little more than half the age of his senior partners, and driving a liquid bomb was definitely a young man's job.

"A young *single* man's job," Buddy corrected him.

"Well, I'm as good as," Hank reminded the other man unhappily.

In fact, Hank and his wife had barely spoken a word to each other in the three months since he had moved into the motel. Of course, there were a lot of things that they needed to talk about. Unfortunately, none of them was pleasant, so they chose to limit their conversations to terse comments and requests regarding their children.

"Hank, would you please explain to Kim that I did not kick you out?"

"Sure, Susan. If you'll get Jake to quit treating me like a leper."

But neither seemed able to do anything with their mutual offspring. Jake continued to ignore his father, while Kim demanded that Hank find an apartment or a house where she could come live with him.

"Why are you still staying in that dump, Dad?" his daughter asked every time she saw him.

"It's cheap," Hank would answer before swiftly changing the subject.

If nothing else, Room 14 was that. From the sagging mattress to the worn indoor-outdoor carpet to the seldom-functioning central heat- and air-conditioning unit, the Carriage Motel was cheap. Even now, as he lay on the bed, Hank could feel the chill seeping through his numerous layers of winter clothing.

Hell, he would have been better off sleeping in the truck, Hank decided as shivers shook his massive frame. Reluctantly he raised his eyelids, knowing that he would never be able to get the sleep he desperately needed.

He lifted his left wrist to a level where his bloodshot eyes could read the watch's little hand. It was only eleven o'clock. He had finished work early tonight. Early enough to go to the front desk and blast his skinflint innkeeper for not getting the heater fixed.

His third pounding on the Ring For Service bell was answered by the whir of rubber wheels rolling across the flat-weave rug as Jackson Talbot maneuvered his wheelchair into the motel office.

"When are you going to turn up the damned thermostat?" Hank growled without preamble. "I'm freezing my tail off in that icebox you rented me."

Talbot merely shrugged his shoulders. "Heater can't do a thing against this kind of weather. It's twenty below with the windchill factor. Southern walls just weren't built to handle a cold spell like this."

Hank knew that, for once, the man had a legitimate defense. Everyone he had talked to tonight had said what amounted to the same thing. His customers kept turning their thermostats up but the only thing they accomplished was burning more fuel and dragging him back out into the cold to refill their propane tanks.

"Well, you can at least give me a few more of those worn hankies that pass for blankets around here," Hank grumbled.

Talbot chuckled at the mild insult. "Sure, anything for my best guest. Help yourself. They're in the closet behind you."

Metcalf turned to get them, then hesitated. "No extra charge?" he asked suspiciously.

His host's grin spread farther across his lean, scarred face. "On the house."

"Well, that's a first," Hank muttered. "You charge for everything else around here."

"Just doing business. You should understand that."

When Metcalf chose to concentrate on getting an armload of covers from the linen closet instead of an answer, Talbot took pity.

"Say, Hank, why don't you head over to the Jube if it's warmth you're looking for? There's enough body heat in there on a Saturday night to keep you warm at forty below. And who knows. With a little luck, you might even get to bring some of it back with you." Talbot shot a conspiratorial grin at the other man. "A hot woman would do you a lot more good than those blankets."

Metcalf almost suggested that the innkeeper take his own advice, but his mouth snapped closed before the words took form. He had no idea whether a man in Talbot's condition could take advantage of a hot woman. Flustered by the thought, he mumbled something indiscernible and hurriedly went back to his room.

He stretched out on the bed again, pulling the mountain of covers up to his chin. When the chill snuck under the blankets with him, Hank closed his eyes and thought as hard as he could about anything warm....

The August sun scorching his shoulders as he sets irrigation pipes in a dusty field.

Camp-fire flames licking at his fingers as he demonstrates proper fire-building techniques to Kim's cadet troop.

Whiskey blazing past a throat left raw from cheering the Arkansas State Indians on to victory from his seat, front and center, before the Jube's wide-screen television.

Susan's buttocks pressing firmly against his loins as they nestle, spoonlike, in the quiet, still hours before children stir and work beckons....

"Susan." An involuntary moan followed her name. His pulse began to quicken. Blood surged through his veins and, at last, Hank felt warm again. Instinct warned him to cut off the fantasy before things got too hot, but desire was already recalling familiar love scenes.

Images flooded in, crowding out the warnings. Hank couldn't shut them off. Intimate details seeped out of traitorous memories and filled his fantasy with shape and sound, scent and texture....

For a brief moment, he is able to hold her again, to love her again. It is only a foolish dream, but for one soul-shattering minute, she is lying beside him once more.

His large callused hands slide around her quiet form, his palms cradling the delicate softness of her breasts. Her head falls back against his chest, dark curls spilling across his shoulder leaving the smooth white curve of her neck exposed for his pleasure. Hungrily his mouth moves across her flesh, his strong teeth nipping gently at her lobe.

"Hank . . ." She purrs his name sleepily—half in protest, half pleading.

He releases the gentle weight of her breasts for a moment, as if he were debating which emotion he should adhere to. But there's really no choice. His hands glide farther down to close over her hips, tugging backward, allowing his arousal to win a snug space between her soft inner thighs. His own heavily muscled leg wraps over hers, securing his advance.

"Hank..." He hears surrender in her voice this time. And acceptance.

Free to resume his exploration with a clear conscience, his skilled, experienced fingers retrace their journey, carefully maneuvering from the valleys to the rise, plucking a response from the gradually hardening tips of her breasts.

"Hank..." Her voice is eager now, encouraging. Her body stretches, sliding sensually against him. Her thighs squeeze around his jutting appendage, her feminine dew moistening its tip.

He retreats, but only to regroup. She turns to watch his every move, exposing herself to a full frontal assault. She is vulnerable but she fears not. Her legs open willingly. Her arms spread out to receive him, closing around his back.

"*Now*," she commands him. "*Now, Hank*."

He thrusts forward, pressing home. "Susan . . . !"

Hank shuddered violently as his lover's name filled the air. He swung his legs over the side of the bed and surged to his feet. Heedless of the bedclothes he left trampled on the floor, he pushed himself into the cold bathroom, stripping off his many layers of clothing on the way. Wrenching the C knob all the way, he stumbled into the shower and let the frigid water cascade over his body, dousing the flames of desire he had foolishly awakened.

He stood under the spray for what seemed an eternity. Finally, the cold began to penetrate and Hank's fiery passion gave way to a sporadic sizzle. He shut off the water, stepped out of the tub and let the freezing air cool the last dying embers.

His breathing gradually calmed, his pulse slowed to the steady cadence of a funeral march. Hank dried himself with a threadbare towel and walked back into the main room with the stringy cloth clutched around his waist. It only took one quick glance at the rumpled bed to confirm that sleep would never be his tonight. His gaze moved on to make a quick search of the room and finally came to a stop at the small indention that served as a closet in the no-frills accommodations.

Maybe Talbot had had the best idea, after all. Hank had been deliberately avoiding the Jubilee since his narrow escape from Sandra Kellogg, but there was no point in avoiding the place forever. All his friends went there. It was the only affordable club in town.

By the time he had tugged on a clean shirt and a decent pair of jeans, Hank had himself convinced. Staying away from the Jube this long probably hadn't even been necessary. After all, the country club was usually more Sandra's style. She must have just been slumming that night in August.

Besides, he told himself, even if she was there, it was highly unlikely she was still interested in him. So why should he deprive himself of a good stiff drink and a roomful of body heat? He couldn't think of a single, solitary reason.

For the first time in weeks, Hank felt a small measure of enthusiasm. Even the arctic blast he received as
he dashed from the motel to his truck couldn't put a
chill on his mood. His mind was made up. Nothing was
going to change it now. A Saturday-night drink with
the boys was just the thing for a cold, lonely working
man separated from his family.

A shouted "Hey stranger!" met him just inside the
Jube's front entrance and Hank easily traced the voice
to a big, burly man perched on a bar stool two sizes two
small for his wide rear end.

The man's neighbors at the bar issued a chorus of
"Hey, Hank!" and "Where've you been, Metcalf? Long
time, no see."

"I've been working," Hank answered easily.

"You mean Joe and Buddy finally got smart and
kicked you out?" asked Junior Bowen, the man who
had spotted him first. "Well, that's tough luck, Hank."

"Yeah, that's a shame, Metcalf," Mike Randall
added. "I hope you didn't have too much trouble finding a real job. After all, there probably aren't too many
people who'll pay someone to drive around in a fancy
white truck and collect gossip."

Hank claimed one of the few empty stools and lowered his voice to a pseudo whisper. "You never know,
boys. I might just decide to go into a new business for
myself. Some of that gossip could be damned profit-
able, you know."

The boys all laughed and slapped him on the back.
"Better watch out, fellows," Junior warned the gathering pack. "He's probably got something on all of us."

As the men settled back down into their standard
routine of jokes and bets and petty arguments, Hank
felt himself begin to relax. He took a draft from Beau,

the bartender, and let the smooth brew ease its way down his throat in one long continuous swallow.

"Look out, Beau," a new voice warned the man behind the bar. "It looks like you've got one thirsty boy here. Go ahead and give him another on me."

Hank eyed Tanner McNeil suspiciously, but let the bartender refill his glass. "What do you need, McNeil?"

"Not a thing, Metcalf. Not a thing. At least, nothing right now," the other man amended with a sly wink.

"Yeah, that sounds more like it," Hank drawled. He took a swig of the beer, fully prepared to pay its price whenever Tanner decided to collect. The good-ol'-boy system hadn't changed a bit during his self-imposed exile from the Jube. It was good to know that. At a time when everything in his life seemed to be going haywire, it was good to know that some things stayed the same.

Tanner's grin disappeared and an unexpectedly somber expression settled on the farmer's face. Turning his back on the rest of the boys, McNeil leaned closer and patted Hank's shoulder with a gentleness that belied his size. "Seriously, Metcalf," he whispered soberly, "I just thought I'd offer you a little drink and the opportunity to commiserate. Misery loves company and all that."

Hank's body began to tense instantly. Tanner could feel the muscles tightening, gathering strength beneath his fleshy palm. "Now, take it easy. I don't mean to pry or nothing. I just wanted to offer my condolences and a sympathetic ear. That's all."

"I don't need anybody's sympathy," Metcalf growled back.

"Sure, you do," Tanner said. "Getting kicked out of his castle is hard on any man. You're no different, Hank. And you're not alone. I can vouch for that."

Hank shook his head furiously. "I wasn't kicked out of anyplace, you old goat. You don't know anything about it. And I strongly suggest you keep it that way."

"Sure, sure," the farmer placated him. "You're right. I don't know the whys, the whens or the what-fors. But I do know you aren't sleeping in your own bed, Hank Metcalf. The whole town knows that. Pretending any different doesn't make it so."

Storm warnings rolled across Hank's face. Tanner's patting became decidedly more forceful. "Now, don't get all riled," he said. "Nobody's trying to criticize or tell you what to do. I'm just trying to tell you that I'm here if you want to talk. That's all. Now, I won't say another word about it. All right?"

Hank nodded briskly, not trusting himself to speak. He was a proud man and a private one. And though he knew McNeil had the best of intentions, he suddenly felt as if he had been thrust stark naked into a room stuffed with fully clothed strangers.

He forced himself to finish the second beer slowly, waiting for just the right moment to make an escape. He had to be careful. The last thing he needed was to expose himself even more.

Finally, McNeil mumbled something about seeing a man about a horse. While his guard headed for the men's room, Hank quietly eased away from the bar and began to slide discreetly toward the red neon Exit sign.

He was halfway there when a cold, sharp-edged grasp took possession of his left arm. Hank turned, expecting to find a tenacious McNeil ready to lead him back for another round. If only he had been so lucky.

"Hello, Hank." Sandra Kellogg edged closer.

"Sandra." Her name came out as much a curse as an acknowledgment, and its harshness caused the woman to draw back slightly.

"I've been wanting to talk to you," the voluptuous blonde continued bravely. "But you haven't been easy to find." She hesitated. A stranger might have thought the woman less than sure of herself. Then Sandra laughed quietly, almost to herself, as if an absurd little thought had suddenly strayed into her head. She looked coyly up at Hank. "Why, one might actually think you had been hiding from me."

Hank stood stiff and straight. "No."

Sandra waited for him to go on but her prisoner offered nothing else. "Well, I guess it doesn't matter. We're both here now." She laughed again and smiled conspiratorially. "I think this is where someone is supposed to say, 'We've got to stop meeting like this.'"

Hank didn't smile back. His mouth was set in a grim, straight line as immobile as one of the famous profiles carved into the side of Mount Rushmore.

"Well, anyway," Sandra continued, "the important thing is that we have run into each other again. Now, maybe we'll have a chance to take up where we left off."

"No."

Sandra frowned at his monosyllabic reply and tugged at the arm she still clutched in exasperation. "Oh, Hank. Don't be that way. I thought we were getting to be pretty good friends last summer. Not as good as we could have if you hadn't left in such a hurry that night, but . . ."

"No." Hank repeated the word slowly and distinctly, shaking off her soft white hands as he spoke. "No. No. No." When she looked up at him with damp blue eyes and pouting lips, he only elaborated on his negative theme. "We're not meeting here. We're not meeting anywhere. We're not friends. We're never going to be friends. We're never going to be anything to each other. Got that?"

Sandra pulled back, stunned by the unexpected hostility emanating from the man she had considered a hot prospect. Her delicate pout changed to a frown as she struggled to find some ploy to overcome this unexpected setback.

"Now, Hank, you don't mean that," she began weakly.

"The hell I don't."

Sandra gasped. "But I thought, I mean—"

"You thought wrong," Hank interrupted. "And as far as that goes, you shouldn't be thinking about other women's husbands at all."

"Well, you sure have changed your tune, haven't you, Hank Metcalf?" Sandra sputtered furiously. "You sure weren't preaching fidelity when you came home with me a few months ago."

"I haven't changed. That night was a mistake. It never would have happened if Susan hadn't— Oh, hell, just forget it, okay? Forget that night ever even happened."

"Fine with me," Sandra agreed too quickly. The porcelain-smooth skin covering her face stretched tight, giving a brittle expression to her finely etched features. "After all, it's not as if there was much to be remembered. I wouldn't have been tempted, either, if I'd known you couldn't deliver. I'll be delighted to leave you and your problem to Susan."

Rage and humility stained Hank's tanned cheeks a crimson red. "The only problem I had that night was the woman I was with," he retaliated. "Maybe if you'd learn to show a little more feeling and do a lot less acting, Sandra, you wouldn't be looking for husband number four."

A loud thwack rolled across the room like thunder as Sandra slapped Hank with every ounce of strength she possessed. The sound echoed endlessly as a sudden, stark silence fell over the crowd.

Simultaneously, the sparring couple realized their very private skirmish was being carried out in a very public place. At least fifty pairs of eyes and ears were tuned in to see and hear what would happen next. They didn't have to wait long.

Sandra burst into tears and ran from the bar as Hank stood staring helplessly around him. A dozen versions of the scene were already circulating in whispers around the room. Swearing angrily at himself, Hank made his own exit.

He was so intent on escaping, he almost tripped over Sandra, sprawled on all fours just outside the door, pawing through the spilt contents of her purse. The woman was too blinded by tears to spot the keys she was searching for, but Metcalf caught the glint of light reflecting off metal and snatched the fourteen-karat heart-shaped key chain from the ground.

"Give them to me!" Sandra leaped to her feet and lunged for the keys, but Hank shook his head, lifting them out of her reach.

"Not until you calm down," he told her grimly. As much as he wished her out of his sight, he didn't wish her dead. "You'd wind up killing yourself if you drove off in this condition."

"So what?" Sandra snarled at him. "Good riddance, wouldn't you say? Isn't that what they would all say?"

"No, that's not what I'd say, and who cares what anybody else says?" Hank snarled back at her. "You were right. Nobody forced me to go home with you. Nobody ever forced any man to cheat on his wife."

"But they will all blame me!" the notorious other woman protested. "You know what those people in there are thinking? A lovers' quarrel, that's what. Isn't that a laugh?" But neither of them was laughing.

"They'll never believe nothing happened between us," Sandra told him. "They think they know it all and at least ten of them are going to call Susan tomorrow and tell her we're having an affair. 'Just another marriage broken up by the happy homewrecker.' That's what they'll say."

Hank shook his head. "You don't know that."

"Oh, don't I?" Sandra scoffed. "You forget, Metcalf, I've played this role before. Hell, if you hadn't let your conscience get the best of you, it would have even been true."

A fresh flood of color stained his face, but Hank shook his head again. "It didn't take an affair or another woman to ruin my marriage," he said quietly. "Things haven't been right between me and Susan for a long time."

Sandra stared at him in surprise, forgetting her own miserable problems for the moment. "It's true, then. You and Susan really are finished?"

It was the question Hank had been avoiding for weeks.

"Hank, are you and Susan really through?" Sandra asked again.

"Yeah," he said finally. "Yeah, I guess we are."

"But why? I mean, did that night in August have anything to do with it? Did someone tell Susan you went home with me?"

"Nobody had to. She saw me leaving your house."

"She what! But how?"

"It doesn't matter. It wasn't your fault. If anybody suggests it is, just tell them to go to hell."

"But didn't you tell her nothing happened? That we didn't actually, you know, sleep together?"

Hank shook his head. "What good would it have done? She wouldn't have believed me anyway."

"Well, then, I'll tell her. She'll have to believe me."

"No!" Startled by his own vehemence, Hank lowered his voice. "Look, just let me handle it, okay? Telling her the truth wouldn't matter, anyway. Like I said, things haven't been right between us for a long time. If it took something like this to make us finally admit it— well, then, so be it."

"You're making a big mistake, Hank."

"Maybe," he admitted. "But that's my problem. And like you said in there, you should just leave my problems for me and Susan to handle."

A blush crept over her pale cheeks. "Hank, I'm sorry about that. I shouldn't have said what I did. We both know it wasn't anything physical that stopped you from going to bed with me."

Hank shuffled awkwardly in place. "Yeah, well, I shouldn't have said what I did, either."

"Forget it. They say the truth never hurts anyone."

"Sandra—"

"No, I mean it, Hank. Just forget it." She held her hand out parallel to the asphalt. "Look, I'm fine now. Not even a tremor. How about letting me get out of this place, before those good folks decide to come out here for act two."

As Hank immediately glanced around for signs of an unwanted audience, Sandra stole her keys back. She had her car door halfway closed when Hank caught it and kept it open.

"Are you sure you're okay now?" he asked.

"I'm fine," she assured him. "But I still think you should tell Susan the truth."

"No."

"Well, do it for my sake if not yours," Sandra urged him, forcing a wry smile. "I don't need any more help ruining my reputation, you know. I've had quite enough already."

"I'll keep that in mind."

"That's it, then." Sandra hesitated a second as he released his grip. "Hank, if you do need someone, just to talk to I mean, you know how to reach me. I'm an expert on surviving divorce."

Divorce? Hank shuddered. What an ugly word. No wonder he had been avoiding even the thought of it. "Yeah, thanks," he muttered as he waved her off.

He glanced wistfully at the club after she had gone. There was nothing he would have liked better at the moment than a shot of whiskey, but he wasn't about to go back inside the Jubilee. With a weary sigh, Hank turned to his own vehicle, tugging his collar up around his ears as he once more became aware of the bitter cold.

5

THE FIRST SUNDAY in December, Susan was feeling rather proud of herself as she paused before the door leading into her Sunday-school class. Three months ago, aware that the whole town was talking about Hank's move into the Carriage Motel, she had barely been able to force herself to walk into that room filled with all-knowing women. Now, she turned the knob and stepped in with confidence, sure that she had given them absolutely nothing to pity her for.

The chatter quieted as she made her entrance but quickly rose back to its previous volume as Susan took the seat Karen Randall and Linda Bowen had saved for her. She suspected from their bright eyes and wide smiles that a new source of gossip must have been found. Well, she'd just have to tell them she wasn't interested, Susan told herself silently. Nothing but hard news for her from now on.

Then Karen reached over and patted her hand enthusiastically. "Oh, Susan. I'm so happy for you. You'll have things back to normal in no time now."

"That's right," Linda chimed in with her own congratulations. "That'll show that shameless hussy not to fool around with our men."

A wave of nausea swept over Susan as the two women continued. "Hold on," she begged them finally. "What are you talking about? What do you mean?"

"Why, that it's all over, of course," Linda said. "That silly affair between Hank and Sandra. They broke up last night. And from what I heard, it wasn't her idea."

"That's right," Karen said. "Of course, Hank was a fool to get involved with her in the first place, but at least it didn't take him long to come to his senses."

Susan stared at them in growing horror. "You don't know what you're talking about! You must be wrong."

"Oh, no!" Linda assured her quickly. "Mike and Junior were right there. Heard the whole thing."

Karen watched the color drain from Susan's face. "Oh, dear. Oh, Susan, I'm sorry. We just assumed you knew. I mean, isn't Sandra the reason Hank moved out?"

"How long have you known?" Susan demanded in a hoarse whisper. "How did you find out? Does everybody know?"

"Well, nobody really knew until last night," Linda answered. "And it wasn't as if Junior and Mike were snooping around or anything. Hank and Sandra picked a fight right in the middle of the Jubilee."

"A fight? What are you two talking about?" Susan demanded again.

An uneasy silence was her only answer. Karen and Linda stared at each other, each quietly pleading with the other to take it from there. They were both saved by the appearance of the minister's wife, who promptly brought the class to attention.

Susan was forced to sit quietly through the forty-five-minute lesson on forgiveness. As soon as the group was dismissed, however, she grabbed the two women sitting beside her and forced them back into a far corner of the emptying room. "All right, now. Tell me everything. Do you hear me? Everything."

IT WAS AN OMINOUSLY quiet family that made its way home from church later. Susan tried to act as if it were just another Sunday. She dropped Kim and Jake off at the end of their driveway with instructions to take dinner out to thaw, finish their homework and call her at the office if there were any problems. Her attempt to smile goodbye was ignored by Kim and interpreted all too correctly by Jake.

"Are you okay, Mom? Is there something I can do for you?" he asked worriedly.

"Of course, I'm okay. What a silly question!" Susan lied, struggling to keep her calm, rational facade in place just a little longer. "Now go on inside. I won't be at the office long."

Jake shut his door and stepped back obediently, but stood on the curb watching until his mother's car turned the corner. As she caught one last glimpse of him in her rearview mirror, Susan knew she hadn't been successful at hiding her rage from him.

Thank goodness, the kids were used to her working Sunday afternoons. The guilt she usually felt about the hours away from her family was replaced by relief. She would never have survived an afternoon of "Let's pretend everything's okay." Not after what she had learned from Karen and Linda.

There had been a time when Susan had thought that nothing could be worse than being a very pregnant and just-a-little-married seventeen-year-old living in a small town.

When she had been carrying Kim, she'd felt as if every eye in Morristown were trained on her growing belly and every tongue wagged with the news about the Mitchum girl who had gotten in trouble in the back seat of Hank Metcalf's Plymouth Duster.

Then she got pregnant again, barely two months after giving birth to her daughter, and had to endure the motherly clucks and blatant disapproval that followed each, "But, honey, don't you know better by now?"

She had thought that after surviving that, she could survive anything—until the night she'd caught Hank coming out of Sandra Kellogg's house. In the past three months Susan had discovered that the only thing the Morristown communications network found more exciting than a shotgun wedding was a broken marriage.

Susan shuddered with renewed anger. How dare Hank embarrass her like this! A wave of red color flooded into her face as the humiliation returned in full force. Losing her husband to the likes of Sandra had been bad enough without having it advertised to the entire Saturday-night crowd at the Jube.

"Damn it, Hank!" She cursed her absent spouse. "You kept the affair quiet. Couldn't you break up with her quietly, too?"

Susan shook her head. Of course, he couldn't. And why should he? He wasn't the one people would be pitying or snickering about. The man never was. "Boys will be boys." That's all anyone would say about a thirty-three-year-old man who strayed from his marriage bed. It was always the wife that received the blame.

"You should have kept a closer eye on him," she'd already been advised several times. "You should have kept him happy. A dog's bound to stray when he's not fed at home."

Well, as far as she was concerned, it was time to put one particular stray to sleep. When Susan entered the *Gazette*'s office she marched straight to the phone and punched in Lara Jamison's number. Lara was just the kind of dogcatcher she needed—a divorce attorney.

"What a coincidence!" Lara exclaimed as she identified the caller. "I was planning to call you this afternoon."

Susan winced. She didn't need two guesses to figure out what the lawyer had wanted to talk to her about. "You must have gone to church this morning."

"Well, yes," Lara admitted.

"Then I suspect you have a pretty good idea why I called." When the other woman failed to volunteer an answer, Susan prodded suspiciously, "You do know, don't you?"

The attorney hesitated a moment. "You mean about the little scene last night at the Jubilee?"

"That's what I mean." Hank's wife sighed. "I guess everyone who went to church this morning knows about it by now."

"Is that how you found out, at church?"

"Yes," Susan said. "Karen and Linda are in my Sunday-school class. Apparently, both their husbands had front-row seats to the Jube's main event."

"I'm sorry, Susan. I know it must have been hard to have something like that hit you unexpectedly. I was hoping Hank might have gotten to you before anyone else broke the news."

"Why should he have?" Susan scoffed. "We've barely spoken since we broke the news to the kids. I don't suppose he felt he owed me any sort of explanation now."

"But if he and Sandra broke up—"

"Not you, too!" Susan almost jerked the phone off the desk. "It didn't surprise me that Karen and Linda expected me to welcome Hank back with open arms now that his little fling is over, but I would never have guessed you'd feel that way, Lara. You're supposed to be on my side."

"I am on your side, Susan," Lara quickly assured her friend and client. "You know I am. But I've handled a lot of divorces. Enough to know that reconciliations under these circumstances aren't at all unusual."

"Are you kidding?" Susan asked incredulously. "I wouldn't even consider it!"

"Well, you should, then. I mean it, Susan," the lawyer added as the other woman began to sputter vehement protests. "I know you've already talked to me about filing for divorce, but there's no reason you can't change your mind. If Hank and Sandra really are through, maybe you could still work things out. At the least, you could try seeing a counselor."

"No!" Susan spoke adamantly. "It wouldn't do any good. Counseling can't erase what's already happened. You can't seriously expect me to just forget the whole thing."

"Of course, I don't," Lara said. "And if you can't forgive Hank, then I agree divorce is your only solution. I just want you to be sure that's what you want."

"I'm positive," Susan insisted. "It's been almost four months since Hank moved out and things have only gone from bad to worse. At least after we're divorced, he won't be able to embarrass me with any more scenes like the one in the Jube last night. The only reason I put off filing this long is because I was hoping to let all the gossip die down." She snorted derisively. "Obviously that was a big mistake. Now all I want to do is get the whole thing over with and get on with my life."

"What about Kim and Jake?" Lara asked gently.

"They are still divided into enemy camps. Kim blames me and Jake blames Hank. Stalling the legal procedures can't make things any better. Maybe when the divorce is final, the kids will at least stop taking sides."

"I assume you want custody?"

"Of course."

"You realize there could be a problem with Kim. She's old enough for the court to allow her some say in who she goes with. If she insists on going with Hank and he agrees, the court will probably go along."

Susan clenched the receiver tightly. "But Hank has agreed that they should stay with me."

"For now," Lara reminded her. "But he isn't going to stay in that motel forever. Once he has a suitable place to live, he might change his mind."

"No. He wouldn't do that to me. Surely, he won't fight me for custody." But she didn't sound convincing even to herself.

"Look, I have a suggestion for you." Lara offered her advice cautiously: "It might not work, but if it did, it would make things a lot easier for all of you, especially the kids."

"Go ahead. I'm listening."

"I want you to consider using divorce mediation. That's how I handled my own divorce and I think it made things a lot easier. However, it will only work if you and Hank are able to sit down long enough to discuss the issues."

"That's asking a lot," Susan said. "We're not speaking."

"I know," Lara said. "But you're going to have to start talking to each other, for the children's sake if nothing else. And if you can work out the separation details between yourselves, mediation will save you a ton in legal bills. You'll also be setting a good example for Kim and Jake."

"Mediation?" Susan repeated skeptically.

"Yes. Basically it means that you and Hank do all of the negotiating instead of hiring attorneys to do it for you. I or another attorney can advise you on the legal details. It cuts your costs to at least half, just by eliminating one legal fee."

Susan sighed. "Exactly how much is there to be worked out in this agreement?"

"Well, custody, of course. Also, child support, the division of property, and who's to be responsible for what debts. Believe me," Lara said, "there is always more than you think there will be."

"I'm not sure if we can do it," Susan confessed. "But, financially we might not have much choice. I don't know if Hank will go for it, though."

"It's okay if Hank wants to use another lawyer," Lara assured her. "I'll be happy to recommend someone else who's also had training in mediation."

"Nonsense!"

"No, I mean it," the attorney said. "I can understand if he would rather use someone he felt might be less biased."

"I'm sure he wants to get this over with just as quickly and cheaply as possible," Susan told her. "He'll go along with the plan and with you."

"Well, if he does, give me a call. I'll brief you on what decisions need to be made and give you some sample agreements to help guide you. You and Hank should be able to take over from there."

"Thanks, Lara. I appreciate your time. Just put this on the bill."

"No way. We'll chalk this up as a little friendly advice." She brushed Susan's protests aside. "No, I mean it. I don't ever want you to hesitate to call me. I've been through a divorce myself, remember. It may seem intolerable at the moment, but you'll survive, Susan. We all survive. Friends just make it a little easier."

Surviving, Susan thought, as she finished up her work at the *Gazette*. That seemed to sum up her whole existence. The paper was just barely staying above the break-even line. The kids were just barely being civil to each other. Her whole world seemed to be hovering precariously on an edge and she had no idea what lay over the precipice, should she fall off.

She drove home slowly, savoring the last few moments she had to herself. Her hand automatically shifted into Park as the car eased to a halt in the driveway, but her body stalled when she tried to open the driver's door.

Susan sat back for a moment, staring at the two-story white clapboard house, dreading going inside now even more than she had the first time she had walked through that front door. Ten years ago, the face created by the front porch and upstairs windows had been anything but welcoming.

Hank had assured her that with a few buckets of paint and a handful of nails the place would suit her just fine. She'd almost told her husband that the house they were renting already suited her just fine and *it* didn't need a thing. But she had held her tongue when she saw the look of pride on his face. If owning the roof over their heads meant that much to Hank, she wasn't going to be the one to point out that it was missing more than a few shingles.

Susan shook her head, smiling in spite of herself. The house would have made a great before-and-after ad. Even she found the transformation miraculous, despite the fact that she'd been there through all the years of repairs and refurbishing.

Of course, the roof still leaked, she reminded herself. And numerous drafts made heating the monstrosity impossible. Still, it had been a home to take pride in. A year ago, she couldn't have imagined abandoning it to strangers.

They'd have to sell the house. That was one of the few decisions that Susan had already made. Economically, she and Hank would have no choice. Aside from finances, she couldn't wait to exchange what had become hostile territory for neutral ground.

Wishing futilely for a camouflage helmet and flak jacket, Susan abandoned the shelter of the car and threw herself into the combat zone that existed where the home used to be.

"Hi, Mom!" Jake jumped out of his chair, dropping the book he was reading to the floor and hurrying to give his mother a hug that would have embarrassed him terribly just a few months before.

Rallied by her troop of one, Susan plunged into the enemy camp as she spied her daughter ensconced on the couch with a thick textbook. "How about you, Kim? How's American history going?"

A smoldering glare was the only response. "What about your science project? Did you get it finished?"

Kim gave her mother a cold shoulder and returned her dark eyes to the homework assignment in front of her.

"Well, I'm glad things are going so well for you." Susan carried on as if they were actually speaking to each other. "Now, how about taking your feet off the couch and putting them on the floor where they belong."

The teenager drew her knees up closer to her chest, dragging her high-top sneakers across the upholstery.

"I said, feet on the floor, Kim. Now." She might not be able to force the girl to be civil to her, but Susan wasn't going to tolerate out-and-out disobedience. Her daughter shot her another glare but the rubber soles slid down to the carpet.

"Thank you. Did either of you remember to take the roast out to thaw?"

"I did," Jake answered quickly. "I peeled the potatoes and chopped the carrots, too. Everything's cooking."

Susan peered inside the oven for confirmation. The roast was browning nicely inside the roasting bag, along with a healthy allowance of vegetables. "Jacob, some woman is going to be very grateful to me someday."

Her son blushed delightfully. "Aww, Mom."

Susan laughed. "Trust me on this. Kim, how about setting the table?"

"Get Jake to do it. Some woman will be grateful to you someday."

Her mother was not amused. "I asked you to do it, Kim. Jake got dinner started. It won't hurt you to help out, too."

"Sorry." Kim didn't sound as if she meant it. "I thought only the men were supposed to do housework around here. I mean, Dad always did it before. Now, you have Jake doing it for you." She shrugged her broad shoulders at the older woman. "I was only following your example, Mother."

She should have been used to the digs by now, but they still hurt. "Just do it, Kim, and spare me the editorial comments."

Somehow the china withstood its sharp impact against the wooden table. Susan winced as she heard each clatter of a plate being slung carelessly down. She bit her tongue against the sharp criticism that threatened to escape. Last time she'd said something, two plates had been instantly broken.

Things couldn't go on like this, Susan thought for the thousandth time. This time, however, the thought progressed a step further. "Set four places, Kim."

Kim looked up, surprised. "Who's coming?"

"Your father, I hope."

"Daddy!"

"Don't get excited. I haven't asked him yet."

"Why are you asking him at all?" Jake demanded.

His mother placed a steadying hand on his shoulder. "We need to discuss a few things, that's all. There's nothing for either of you to get excited about. In fact, don't you two have a youth-group meeting to attend tonight?"

"That's okay, we don't need to go," Kim announced.

"Oh, yes, you do."

"But I want to see Dad."

"I know, but I need to talk to him privately. Now, don't start huffing and puffing, Kim. I'll save our conversation till after you two leave for church. You'll be able to talk to him all you want during dinner. At least, you will if he doesn't have other plans."

"He won't. I'll go call him right now."

Kim dialed the number before her mother could protest and, on second thought, Susan decided it was just as well. Hank was far more likely to respond to an invitation from his daughter than from his wife.

She held her breath as she heard "Daddy's little girl" pulling all the strings. It took a little wheedling, but Kim was flushed with triumph when the receiver was placed back on its hook. "He's coming!"

Her daughter flew into action then. "Come on, y'all. Let's clean this place up! Take your books upstairs, Jake."

"What for? It's just him. It's not like we're expecting anyone important."

"Just do it," Kim ordered her little brother. "Mom, tell him."

"Oh, for Pete's sake, Kim. Your father lived here for thirteen years. He knows what the place usually looks like."

"But—"

"Kim, honey, he's just coming to dinner. That's all."

"Well, maybe if you'd start acting more like a wife and mother, that wouldn't be all." Kim stomped her foot and threw her hands in the air in frustration. "Why can't you just be like other women?"

"Because she's a lot better than other women!" Jake retorted. "Why should she be anything else when she's already the best?"

"Who says so?" Kim demanded angrily. "Not me. For once I'd like a mother like everyone else has."

"And exactly what do other wives and mothers do that I don't, Kim? Tell me that." Susan grabbed her daughter by the arms and forced the girl to face her. A crack had finally emerged in the wall of silence that had been building between them. She'd be damned if she was going to let Kim seal it back up without finding out exactly why her daughter had turned against her.

"They stay home," Kim answered readily. "They clean house and cook and go shopping. They don't miss birthday parties or Thanksgiving dinners because of a fire or some stupid political speech. Other mothers don't put their jobs ahead of their families. Other wives don't leave their husbands alone at night so that they end up going to some other woman for what they should be getting at home."

Susan dropped her hands in shock. "You know?" She stared from one child to the other. Their faces said it all. "You both know."

Jake shuffled his feet uneasily. "The other kids heard their parents talking about the fight he had with Sandra at the Jubilee. By now, everybody in town knows Dad was cheating on us."

"Not us," Kim objected. "Just her. And it's her own fault."

"Bullsh—!"

"Jake!"

"Well, that's what it is," Jake said unrepentantly. "Dad was jealous because you're more important than he is. He cheated on us so you'd be jealous, too. It's all his fault."

"You're the one that is full of—" Kim turned on her brother furiously, but was checked instantly by Susan.

"Stop it, both of you!" Their mother slumped onto the nearest chair and buried her face in her hands. The sight of the strong, capable woman reduced to tears silenced both children.

"Mom, don't cry." Jake stood beside her, gently patting her back, terribly unsure what else to do. Kim said nothing and sank down onto another chair as if she, too, had been robbed of all her strength.

"I'm sorry," Susan whispered finally. "I just wanted to make things as easy for the two of you as possible."

"You should have told us the truth, then," Kim scolded.

"Honey, I don't know what the truth is anymore. Only your father and Sandra know exactly what happened between them, and they're not talking. As for who's to blame, well, I guess, your dad and I take equal credit. We both made mistakes."

Kim's chin began to wobble uncontrollably. "But if you just stayed home more, if you hadn't bought the newspaper..."

"Don't you think I've thought about that, Kim? Over and over again. But what if I hadn't? Even when I was just working as a reporter I still had to work late. It would have happened eventually."

"You don't know that," her daughter protested.

Susan shook her head. "It's beside the point now, anyway. Look, the fact is that your father and I have had problems for a long time and we were all ignoring them. If things had been okay, then none of this would have happened."

Kim crossed her arms and sat up rigidly, every bit as unmovable as her father. "I still say there wouldn't have been any problems if it weren't for the newspaper."

"That's ridiculous." Jake drew up a seat for himself and joined the discussion. "You should be proud of Mom and what she's done with the *Gazette*. Everybody's been saying what a great job she's doing. I'm proud of her, and someday I'm going to be just like her."

Susan smiled at her son. He was already so much like her, she ached for him sometimes. But she hurt even more for her daughter whom she was dangerously close to losing. "Kimmie, I'm sorry you don't like what I do, but I can't help that. I am a journalist, honey. I can't change that and I wouldn't, even if I could."

"Of course not, because being a journalist, a publisher, is more important to you than being a wife and mother," Kim said again.

"One isn't more important to me than the other," Susan explained patiently. "But they are all part of who I am. Asking me to be different would be like my insisting that you study ballet instead of playing basketball. Can't you understand that?"

But the girl clammed up again, retreating somewhere inside her thick skull. Just like her father, Susan thought, and wished, for an instant, that she could shake that strong resemblance out. But she couldn't. And even if she could, she wouldn't. People came as they were. Hadn't she been listening to her own lecture?

The sound of Hank's pickup pulling into the drive filled the silence, followed by the slam of his door and the clump of tired feet encased in old boots shuffling up the walk. There was an awkward pause outside the front door and the trio at the table could all read his mind. Should he knock or should he just go in? Was it still his home or was he merely a visitor?

Kim spared them all from having to answer. She ran to the door and threw it open, launching herself into her father's arms.

6

LORD, IT FELT GOOD to hold her. Hank lifted Kim off the floor, swung her in a circle and felt the years melt away. It didn't matter how big or independent she got; three years old, thirteen or thirty, she would always be his baby.

"Now, that's the way to greet your old man." He set the girl back down with a grin, keeping one arm around her as they stepped inside. "Think you can beat that, Jake?"

But Henry Jacob Metcalf, Jr., apparently wasn't willing to try. Neither was his mother. "You did say I was invited, didn't you, Kim?"

"Of course, Dad. Just have a seat. Dinner's almost ready. Come on, Jake. Help me get the table set."

"Little brother" waited for a nod from his mom before complying, but went to work the instant approval came, leaving the field of battle to the two commanders.

Hank pulled out a chair on the opposite side of the table from his wife and sat down heavily. "So what is this about, exactly? Kim said you wanted to talk."

"I do, but not yet. The kids will be going to their youth-group meeting at church right after dinner. Let's wait till after they've left."

"You should have told me that. I would have waited until then to come over."

"Why? We've shared supper hundreds of times. I'm sure that we can survive one more meal together." Susan hesitated as the children came in bearing platters. Her gaze stayed fixed on their backs as they retreated once more to the kitchen and she added meaningfully, "For their sake if nothing else."

"All right," Hank agreed.

An unspoken pact reigned over the meal. Questions and comments were restricted to safe topics focusing on Kim and Jake.

"How's basketball practice going, Kim? . . . Leading in rebounds? . . . Great."

"Jake, how are you doing with that trumpet? . . . First chair, really? . . . That's good."

If their lives had been a film, they could simply have cut out the past few months and no one would ever have guessed at the tragedy lying on the editing-room floor. But it wasn't a movie, and "Let's pretend" ended when the younger generation's ride to church arrived.

Hank immediately dispensed with all the niceties and cut straight to the nitty-gritty. "Okay. I'm here. The kids are gone. What's on your mind?"

"Divorce."

The simple one-word answer hit him hard—so hard it seemed to knock the wind right out of him for a moment. "I thought we agreed there was no hurry."

"That was four months ago."

Hank shrugged. "That's not so long."

"It's been long enough," Susan decreed. "I really don't see a need to delay things any longer."

"But the kids—"

"The kids know everything," she interrupted. "There's no need to spare them. In fact, the kindest thing we could do is get things finalized and allow everyone to get on with their lives."

"What do you mean they know everything? You don't mean—" Susan's nod confirmed his worst fears. "But I thought we agreed not to tell them any details."

"Yes, we did," his wife said. "Unfortunately, you forgot to swear the rest of the town to secrecy, Hank. If you wanted Kim to keep seeing you as the knight in untarnished armor, you should have picked a more private place to fight with your floozy."

Susan laughed at the pained grimace that crossed his face. "Oh, yes, Hank. I heard all about it. Karen Randall and Linda Brown were thrilled to share the news with me. And if I hadn't heard it from them in church this morning, I'm sure I would have learned about it at the hair salon or the grocery store or the gas station. Everyone is always anxious to give the *Gazette's* publisher the latest scoop on her own husband."

Hank winced and shifted uncomfortably in his seat at the head of the table. "Is that what made you decide to go ahead with this thing?"

"It's called a divorce. Just two syllables, Hank. Come on, you can say it."

Her gibe hit harder than she knew. "You don't have to keep treating me like the village idiot, Susan. I may not have your college degree, but that doesn't mean I'm completely ignorant."

"I never said you were," his wife protested in confusion.

"Well, that's what you implied. You'd better watch out yourself, Suz. Save the sharp tongue for the editorials or you'll start to sound like a bitter old woman."

Hank grinned unrepentantly as her soft gasp confirmed his hit. It was a shallow victory but it wasn't often that he got in a good shot when verbally jousting with his wife. Words were her game, not his, which was one good reason why he avoided them as much as possible in her presence.

Susan stared at him in shocked silence until her eyes began to burn. She quickly slipped long, slender fingers beneath her glasses to dash the moisture away. "How on earth did we ever manage to stay together this long?"

The quiet, trembling voice demolished Hank's brief moment of triumph. "Hell, I'm sorry, Susan. It's just that you caught me off guard, that's all. When Kim called and said you wanted me to come over, I thought, well, that is, I thought . . ."

"You thought I was asking you to come back home?" Susan filled in for him. She sighed when he nodded guiltily. "Karen and Linda seemed to think that's what I should do, too. And Lara even suggested that we see a counselor before we go through with legal proceedings."

"Well, then—"

"Well, what?" Susan quickly dashed any hopes Hank might have on that score. "Whatever happened between you and Sandra last night doesn't erase whatever's been happening between you two for the past few months. I don't see why it should make any difference in our filing for a divorce now."

"But that's what last night was all about," Hank said. "The fact that nothing happened. That nothing *ever* happened. Didn't anybody tell you that?"

Susan shook her head in confusion. "I don't know what you're talking about. The only thing I learned was that you and Sandra had words, then she slapped you and left alone."

Hank swore angrily under his breath. "You know, I'd think a journalist with your experience would have learned to get all the facts. Damn it, the whole scene with Sandra at the Jube happened because I wasn't interested in her! I never have been interested in her."

"Then why were you at her house that night?" Susan asked. "If you weren't interested in Sandra, then why the hell did you go home with her?"

"Because I was mad at you," he answered honestly. "It had nothing to do with wanting her. I was just tired of being kept waiting on the back burner while you covered every grass fire in three counties. I went home with Sandra because you wouldn't come home to me. But nothing happened, Susan. I swear nothing happened."

His wife got up so suddenly her chair was sent crashing to the floor. She stood over Hank and stabbed an accusing finger into his chest. "I saw her lipstick on your face. I could smell the scent of her all over you." Susan's eyes filled with tears, her voice cracked with emotion, but she forced herself to go on. "You can't ask me not to believe what I saw with my own eyes."

Hank soared to his feet and loomed threateningly over her, staring down at her through coal-black eyes that glowed with a fire held in check too long. "I don't deny going with Sandra. I'm just saying I didn't make love to her. I couldn't make love to her!" Desperately he clenched his huge hands around her upper arms, hauling Susan up against his chest. "Woman, can't you understand? I didn't want a substitute. I wanted you! If you had just been where you belonged—"

Susan shoved her palms against him, trying to free herself. "I *was* where I belonged!" she insisted furiously. "I was doing my job and I was trying to hurry so

I could go home to my husband. You were the one in the wrong place, Hank Metcalf. You're the one that strayed off-limits!"

"But nothing happened!" Hank tightened his grip, determined to hold on to his wife, but Susan twisted in his arms like a wildcat refusing to be caged. "Susan, you've got to believe me."

"I don't know what to believe anymore." She broke free at last, quickly putting distance between them. "But it doesn't make any difference. Someone who attempts a crime isn't any less guilty just because they failed to succeed. How can I ever trust you now?"

"The same way you trusted me before." Hank tried to close the gap she put between them, but Susan took two steps back for every step he took toward her. He stopped finally and tried one last approach from a safe, nonthreatening distance. "I never let you down before this happened, Susan. Just give me a chance to make things like they used to be."

"No." His wife shook her head sadly. "It can't ever be like it used to be, Hank. You changed everything. There's only one way out of the mess we're in now."

Hank felt the weight of the world sink onto his shoulders. "Divorce?"

"Divorce."

He gulped as he heard her confirmation. "But what about Kim and Jake?"

"They'll adjust," Susan said with a confidence she didn't feel. "And the sooner we get everything settled and done with, the better off they'll be."

Taking a deep breath, she forced her voice into a calm, businesslike monotone. "I've already talked to Lara Jamison about the legalities. She suggested mediation might make things easier and less expensive for both of us. Basically, it means that we work out the details ourselves, using a lawyer as an adviser and a mediator when necessary."

"You're really sure this is what you want?" Hank chanced one small step in her direction. "Won't you even consider—"

"No."

"Fine." He spun on his heel and began marching to the front door. "That's just fine with me. You draw up the papers and I'll sign them."

"But that's not the way it's supposed to work," Susan protested. "Weren't you listening, Hank?"

"Believe me, I heard every single word. But you don't need me to draw up those documents. You seem quite capable of deciding everything all by yourself."

"But the whole point of mediation is to work things out together."

"Wrong," Hank corrected her. "The whole point is to get things over with. You're the writer, so you write it."

He was out the door before she could say anything else. Susan stood rooted in her spot by outrage. Typical. That was just typical of the man. "Well, that's *fine*," she mimicked him to the empty room. "It'll probably work out better like this anyway. The less time I have to spend with you, the better."

First thing Monday morning, Susan stopped by Lara Jamison's office and picked up the sample agreements the lawyer had promised. Anxious to get it all over and done with, she set to work immediately, only to be interrupted by a four-alarm fire.

Like everyone else on staff, Susan wore more than one hat for the *Gazette*. Although officially she was now known as the publisher, she was still serving as the

Gazette's editor and primary hard-news reporter. The only other full-time journalists on staff were her sports editor/reporter and her photo editor/reporter/copy editor. She had two part-timers who contributed feature articles and sold ads, and a part-time photographer who did weddings and graduation pictures on the side. Her secretary made up the entire classified staff and also wrote a weekly "Happenings" column. Her other two employees were kept busy with typesetting and production—an arduous task on the *Gazette*'s antiquated equipment.

Susan was never more aware of her need to hire more help than during the next week. It seemed that the whole town was conspiring against her completing the separation agreement. But she refused to let it rest. The notebook she carried with her at all times was filled with questions for her attorney and accountant, as well as notes to herself.

The brief lull between the completion of the Tuesday edition and the start of Saturday's was spent at the *Gazette*'s sole word-processor, pounding out a rough draft. Susan took the preliminary form to bed with her that night and found herself waking up at odd hours to jot down additions or to double-check the phrasing of a clause. Lara had been right; there was far more to deal with than Susan had dreamed.

By Saturday, dark circles had appeared beneath her eyes and she had shed at least another five pounds, but Susan didn't care. The agreement was finished. She wasted no time in dialing the Farmer's Seed & Supplies' number.

"It's done," she announced without preamble when Hank came on the line.

"Susan?" Hank seemed stunned by the fact that his wife had called. Then her words slowly penetrated. "What's done? What do you mean?"

"The agreement," she clarified impatiently. "It's finished."

"Already? I thought it would take a lot longer than this."

"I've had to work around the clock to get it knocked out, but it's done. All you have to do is sign it. I'll leave a copy at the Carriage's front desk for you. Just take it to Lara after you have it notarized."

"Hold on a second," Hank said. "I think you should be there when I read it, in case I have any questions. I should be able to get away in a couple of hours. Why don't you meet me in my room?"

His suggestion took her by surprise, but Susan decided instantly that there was no way she was going to be stuck alone with Hank Metcalf in a room whose only furnishing was a double bed. "No, I don't think that's necessary. You can just call if you have any questions."

"I thought you were in a hurry to get this settled." When his wife didn't respond, Hank pushed harder. "Come on, Suz. Your mother took the kids to Memphis shopping, didn't she?"

"You know she did," Susan said grudgingly.

"Then, now's the perfect time for us to get together."

"All right, all right," she snapped. "But why don't you come by the house? Or better yet," she amended, with a flash of inspiration, "I'll meet you at Riley's."

"Riley's? Don't you think that's a little public for this kind of meeting?"

"I think it's neutral—just the right setting for this sort of negotiation," Susan said. "I'll meet you there at one o'clock." She hung up quickly before Hank could offer any more arguments, and sighed with relief. Riley's was the perfect answer. Despite the now infamous scene at the Jubilee, Susan knew her husband had an ingrained distaste for publicity.

She arrived at the café half an hour early just to make sure she beat Hank there. She had a vague notion that the arrogant male would turn right around and leave if she wasn't there when he arrived. Susan could tell by the look on Hank's face when he spotted her in the rear corner that that was exactly what he had planned.

The longing backward glance Hank gave his red pickup showed that he was still tempted to make a quick exit. Susan knew it was only his stubborn pride that kept him moving toward her booth.

She waited until Riley had taken their orders before pulling out two copies of the agreement she had drawn up. "I think you'll find everything in order," she reported. "As you'll see when you read it, I've tried to be as thorough as possible."

Hank accepted the surprisingly thick document without comment and silently began to skim the pages. Susan waited confidently until he took a pen out of his pocket and began to edit.

"Hey, hold on a second. What are you doing?"

"In a minute. Let me finish reading first. Then we can go over my changes," Hank said.

Susan fumed. "If you had something to say, you should have helped draw it up. You already forfeited your rights to me."

"The hell I did! I just said you could do the first draft. I didn't say anything about accepting it lock, stock and barrel."

"Well, hurry up then."

Hank shook his head and xed out another paragraph. "Sorry, but I think this is going to take a while."

"Oh, come on!" Susan cried. "You can't find that much to disagree with. This is an exceptionally fair agreement."

Hank had the nerve to laugh. "That obviously depends on who's doing the judging. You can't seriously believe that I'd go along with some of this garbage."

"Like what, for instance?"

"Like you taking sole custody of the kids, for instance."

"But you have unlimited visitation rights."

"I don't want to be a visitor in my children's lives."

"Well, then, you shouldn't have walked out on them."

"I didn't walk out on *them*," Hank spoke distinctly. "I walked out on *you*. Don't get the two confused, Susan. I have no intention of divorcing my children."

"Keep your voice down." She scanned the room for obvious eavesdroppers. Satisfied that their conversation still had a modicum of privacy, Susan shoved her glasses back up and leveled as steady a stare as her wandering left eye was capable of at her soon-to-be ex-husband.

"Look, Hank. This is just a technicality. One of us has to be named legally responsible for them."

"Bull!" He lowered his voice when Susan shushed him again, but he refused to be silenced. "We can both remain their legal guardians. It's called joint custody, in case you didn't know."

Hank shook his index finger in her face. "You probably thought you could get away with pulling a fast one, but not this time. I did my homework for once, Susan. I'm not just a dumb jock these days."

"I wasn't trying to pull anything over on you," she protested. "And what's with the 'dumb jock' bit? That's the second time you've implied I think you're stupid, and I resent it."

"Well, maybe you don't think I'm dumb, but you sure treat me like you do."

"That's not true."

"Isn't it?" Hank insisted. "When did you ever discuss *Gazette* business with me, Susan? Every time I've asked you to share your problems with me, you just shrugged it off and said, 'Oh, you wouldn't understand.' Hell, I own part of a business, too. I may not understand all of it, but I can understand parts. You wouldn't even give me a chance. Hell, you wouldn't even let me deliver the damned newspapers!"

Susan stared at him, horrified by his interpretation of her motives. "I didn't want to bother you, that's all. I thought you'd taken on enough responsibility at home and at the Seed and Supply without me dumping more on your shoulders."

"Yeah, right," Hank muttered under his breath.

"Yes, that's right. Believe me, Hank Metcalf, the only time I've ever questioned your intelligence was when you decided to play the fool with Sandra Kellogg." Susan snatched the separation agreement out of Hank's hands and began to gather her things together.

"I don't know whatever made me think we could work this out between ourselves. It's obvious we have a serious communication problem. Just forget this, Hank. We'll go back to the original plan. Get your own attorney. I'll get mine and we'll argue about your rights all you want."

Hank clamped one large hand around Susan's wrist like a manacle chaining her to the table. "Hold on.

Look, I'm sorry if I misunderstood you. But you misunderstood me, too. I didn't say we couldn't use some of this. There are just going to have to be a few minor changes."

"The question of custody isn't a minor one."

"All right," he relented. "Then make that a few major changes. It's still not anything that we can't work out between ourselves." Hank ignored Susan's unladylike snort. "Look, Susan, even if we hire ourselves a mouthpiece, the final decision still comes down to us. One way or the other, you and I are the ones who have to reach an agreement. Not the lawyers."

This reasonable, rational version of Hank Metcalf threw Susan off base and she hesitated a second too long. Before she could decide what to do, Riley had set two hot-lunch specials down on the table. Leaving now was sure to cause a scene, and more publicity was the last thing the Metcalf family needed. Reluctantly, Susan settled back down, picked up a fork and fastidiously moved food from one side of her plate to the other.

"Eat," Hank ordered.

"I'm not hungry."

"Well, you should be. You look like you haven't eaten in a week. I'll bet you've lost at least fifteen pounds since August and you were too skinny even then."

"I haven't, either. Besides, I'm not too skinny. There's no such thing."

"Bull." Hank nudged her plate closer to her. "Come on, take a few bites and then we'll talk."

Susan found herself responding automatically. This was the Hank she thought she had known—an absurd cross between nurturer and bully. She could feel his black eyes recording each nibble she took, and she savored the warm memory of better times that was stirring to life.

Hank read her mind. A slow smile spread across his rugged face. "It seems like a million years ago, yet it also seems like yesterday."

Susan nodded. "I know. On one hand, I can't believe I was ever seventeen and pregnant. On the other, it doesn't seem possible that I'm over thirty with a thirteen-year-old daughter."

"Lord, you had me scared back then," Hank confessed. "You hardly ever ate and when you did you were always sick. I thought for sure I was going to lose both you and the baby."

"Well, we both made it through. Kim came out strong and healthy. So did Jake." Susan shook her head. "When you think of all the awful things everyone predicted, our lives really didn't turn out so bad, did they?"

"No, they didn't," Hank agreed. "We certainly lasted longer than everybody figured."

"Umm, but not as long as we thought ourselves," Susan said. "We believed in 'forever' back then."

Hank rubbed a calloused finger across his nose and sniffed. "We were young."

"Very." Susan shook her head as if she were just now beginning to understand how young they had been. "Do you realize that Kim will be starting high school next year? Pretty soon she'll be as old as I was when we first started dating."

"Do I realize it? Snookums, I wake up with nightmares about it." Hank shuddered visibly. "The thought of Kim taking up with some kid like I was gives me a whole new respect for your dad. No wonder the poor man had a heart attack."

"Hank! Daddy's heart attack happened years after we married."

"Delayed reaction," he said. "I guarantee we took our toll on his ticker. I remember him telling me the day Kim was born that she was the best revenge he could have gotten."

"Well, if nothing else, maybe our divorce will do a better job of convincing Kim and Jake to wait than our parents' arguments did for us," Susan said.

"Maybe." Hank sounded doubtful. "I don't see how a divorce can possibly be good for children, though. Susan, are you really sure this is what you want?"

His wife blinked in surprise at the sudden change of topic. "What choice do I have, Hank? What choice have you left me? I can't condone what you've done to me, to our family."

"Everybody makes mistakes," Hank said. "Can't we just put it behind us and go back to being a family?"

Susan shook her head. "Pretending nothing happened certainly won't make things any better."

"But if we started over," he insisted. "If you could just spend more time at home . . ."

"Oh, no, you don't!" Susan shoved her unfinished meal away. "You're not putting it all off on me again. How can we start over when you won't even take responsibility for what you've done?"

"But can't you understand?"

"No."

Hank sighed. "Well, I guess that's that, then."

"Yes. The best thing is to get everything finalized, which brings us back to this separation agreement." Susan placed her elbows on the table and steepled her fingers in a no-nonsense posture. "Are you willing to try and work it out ourselves, or not?"

"Considering the alternative, yes."

"If we are going to do it this way, we're going to do it by the book," Susan cautioned him. "I'm not going to stay up nights working out agreements for you to trash in five minutes."

Hank held his hands up in a gesture of surrender. "You're right. That wasn't fair. To be honest with you, I didn't realize I had such strong feelings about things until I started reading your draft." He glanced at his watch. "Look, I don't have time to finish going over it right now. I've still got six more deliveries to make this afternoon."

"Deliveries?"

"Yeah." Hank was already struggling back into his heavy coat. "Billy quit the first of September so I've started driving the propane truck again."

"Hank Metcalf, have you lost your mind? What on earth possessed you to start driving that liquid bomb again?"

Her husband shrugged his shoulders, hiding a pleased smile behind his turned-up collar. "Somebody's got to do it. Since I'm one of the owners, it's my responsibility. You can understand that, can't you?"

His use of her own favorite excuse infuriated Susan, but she refused to let him see how bothered she was. "Yes, yes, I understand. When do you want to get to work on this, then?"

"That's all you have to say?" Hank asked, clearly disappointed.

"It's your life," she told him. "Just be sure you keep your life-insurance policy paid up, for the sake of the kids. Which reminds me, I forgot to put anything in here about who is responsible for the insurance premiums."

Incredulous, Hank watched as Susan whipped out her memo pad and jotted a quick note to herself. When she was finished, she stuck the pen back in her pocket and looked inquiringly at her husband. "So, when do you want to resume negotiations?" she asked.

"What? Oh, yeah, right. Negotiations." Hank shook his head. "I guess tomorrow night. I'll come for dinner and then we can discuss things after the kids leave for church."

It was Susan's turn to stare dumbfounded. "Dinner? Why don't you just come around seven, after Kim and Jake leave?"

"Because we're trying to set a good example for them, remember?"

"Of course, but I don't think that requires having dinner together."

"Why not?" Hank asked. "We got by last Sunday without arguing in front of them. And, we managed to be civil to each other today, didn't we?"

"Yes," she agreed hesitantly. "But we didn't get much accomplished."

Hank smiled. "Oh, I don't know about that."

Susan stared at him with growing suspicion. "What's that supposed to mean?"

Hank adjusted his S&S cap and with a quick salute turned to leave. "You'll see," he promised. "You'll see."

7

THE CONNECTION still exists.

Hank kept a firm grasp on the propane truck's steering wheel, trying not to let his excitement get the best of him. It was way too soon to be celebrating. After all, the "connection" hadn't kept him and Susan from separating. But then, it hadn't been functioning very well around that time.

Come to think of it, Hank realized, *it hasn't been working at all for the past couple of years.* Funny, until he felt it at Riley's, Hank hadn't even been aware the link had been missing. How could they have lost something like that without noticing?

At least they hadn't lost it for good. Their meeting at Riley's proved that. It may have been brief, but the feeling was unmistakable. And Susan had sensed it, too. He was sure of it.

For a few precious seconds, they had felt as one, flashing back to another time. Seventeen and nineteen. On their own. Susan pregnant. Scared. Excited. In love. There were no words exchanged or thoughts transmitted. Only emotion, feelings. Things that couldn't be spoken. Things that could only be felt.

When had they lost that? Hard as he tried over the next few hours, he couldn't remember. As he pulled up at the Carlsons', his last stop of the day, Hank decided to quit trying. When they had lost it wasn't important.

All that mattered was that now they had a chance to get it back.

"Question is," he asked himself as he got out of the cab, "how the hell can we reconnect when we're supposed to be getting a divorce?"

"What's that?" Mrs. Carlson cupped one hand behind her left ear as she waddled toward him, wrapped securely in a heavy blanket, her feet shuffling awkwardly in a pair of boots that obviously belonged to her husband. "Speak a little louder, son. This cold air must not agree with my battery."

"Nothing wrong with your hearing aid, Mrs. Carlson," Hank assured the seventy-eight-year-old woman. "I was just talking to myself."

Her eyebrows shot up in alarm. "Don't do that, son. Someone hears you, they'll cart you off to the old folks' home quicker than lightning."

"Guess I'd better watch myself, then," Hank said and chuckled.

"You do that. And don't forget to come inside for some good hot coffee after you've taken care of business out here. Red's been watching out the window for you all day. I put a fresh pot on as soon as he saw you coming."

Hank's smile fell away instantly. "Uh, I'm afraid I'm going to have to skip it today, ma'am. I'm way behind schedule."

"Nonsense," Mrs. Carlson insisted. "There's always time for a cup of hot coffee. Especially on a day as cold as this."

Out of the corner of his eye, Hank could see lace window curtains twitching. Guiltily, he gave in. It was his last stop and quite likely the only stop anyone had made at the Carlsons' all week, aside from the rural health nurse. "You're right, Mrs. Carlson. There's always time for coffee."

The woman's face lit with relief. "Of course, there is. Now, you just hurry inside so we can get you all warmed up."

"As soon as I get your tank filled," Hank promised.

He kept a smile pasted on until Mrs. Carlson had scurried back inside the tiny house. Then he walked around to the far side of the truck and let go with a stream of curses and a swift kick at the nearest tire. Why the hell had he scheduled the Carlsons for today of all days?

Most of his customers liked to chat. The farther from town they lived, the more so. And the old folks like the Carlsons, they'd just as soon give him a bed and let him move right in.

Usually, Hank enjoyed taking the time to visit. But not today. He had serious business to attend to. Like saving his marriage. Still, there was nothing that could be done about it. He'd never forgive himself if he let Ol' Red down.

But he absolutely was not staying for dinner, Hank promised himself as he finished filling the Carlsons' propane tank and headed for the house. Not this time. His conscience didn't require that much.

"Hullo, Red. You old goat. Whatcha been up to?" Hank pulled up a chair beside the hospital bed that had replaced Mrs. Carlson's Victorian sofa. The unusual location had never fazed Hank. In fact, putting the bed in the living room made pretty good sense to him. A man in Red's condition needed all the positive thinking he could get.

"Been watching for you," Red answered in a wheezy voice. "Knew you'd come today. Told Junebug you would. Didn't I, Junebug?"

"You sure did, Redbird," Mrs. Carlson confirmed as she brought in two mugs of coffee. "This man has always had a feeling for things, Hank. Like that hailstorm back in '39. Remember that? Well, of course you wouldn't, Hank. Oh, but it's a shame. That was one doozy of a storm. Red knew it was coming, but nobody believed him. Go on and tell him about it, Redbird. You haven't heard this before. Have you, Hank?"

Only forty or fifty times. "No, ma'am. I don't believe I have." Hank helped her crank up Red's bed to a sitting position, then sat back to listen as if he'd never heard the tale before. Half an hour later, he quit looking at his watch and started watching the Carlsons very closely.

"How long have you two been married?" he asked as Mrs. Carlson refilled their coffee mugs at the end of yet another story.

"Sixty years next June first," Red answered without prompting. "Haven't forgotten a wedding anniversary yet. Have I, Junebug?"

"Not a one. Course, you'd have to forget my name first."

Red cackled gleefully. "Pretty smart, don't you think, Hank? Picked the date myself. All I've ever had to remember is 'June is my first wife.'"

Hank grinned and gave the old man a conspiratorial wink. "That's great, Red. So what's your second wife's name?"

"Second wife?" Mrs. Carlson sputtered as her husband played right along, holding a quivering finger up to his thin, pale lips as if begging Hank not to give him away.

"Shame on both of you," Junebug scolded when the two men began to laugh. "Any more of that and I won't offer you one piece of that fried chicken I've got waiting in the kitchen."

"I'll be good, I'll be good," Hank quickly assured her, forgetting his promise not to stay.

"Well, I don't know. I'm not so sure I can trust you now."

Hank winced. Women seemed to be losing trust in him on a regular basis these days. "I guess I'll just have to prove myself, then. I noticed a bit of draft around these windows here. How about if I get some of that heavy-duty tape out of the truck and try to eliminate a little of that cold seeping in?"

"Oh, you don't have to do that, hon," Mrs. Carlson protested. "I was just teasing, you know."

"Well, I'm not." Hank was already tugging his coat and hat back on. "I bet I can get these windows fixed up before you can get supper on the table."

"Really, Hank—"

But Metcalf was already out the door.

"Better get moving, Junebug. He's got a good head start on you."

"All right, Redbird. I'm moving."

REDBIRD AND JUNEBUG were still on Hank's mind long after he'd left their house. Sixty years together and they still had that something special. It was obvious in the way they looked at each other, the way they communicated without words.

He and Susan used to be like that. On his way back to his cold, lonely motel room, Hank decided he was going to do his damnedest to get that something special back. Sixty years from now, he wanted his grandchildren to be able to watch him and Susan together and still feel that magical connection. Only they'd be Snookums and . . . and what?

Funny, Hank realized, Susan didn't have a special name for him. She called him by his full name when she was mad, but so did his mother. She called him "honey" and "sweetheart," "dear" and "darling," but those were generic terms. He wanted something special. Hell, she was a writer. She ought to be able to think of something good.

He'd have to work on that when they reconciled. First, he had to get her back, though. Hank had never claimed to be an imaginative man. But he had played enough football in high school to draw up a pretty good game plan.

His defense was obviously his weak spot. Hank wasn't sure he understood all the reasons for his behavior over the past few months. He'd have a devil of time explaining it to someone else.

So, Hank decided, he was just going to have to concentrate on his offense and hope that he could score enough points that he wouldn't have to worry about defending his recent past.

He spent the rest of the night mentally sketching out his playbook. By the time light began to peek through the paper-thin curtains of Room 14, Hank was working diligently on putting his first play into action. He'd even managed to drag his reluctant landlord into the game.

"You got me up at seven o'clock on Sunday morning for a freaking iron?" Jackson Talbot grumbled. "Man, where do you think you're staying? The Ritz? I don't have no twenty-four-hour service and I don't have an iron."

"I figured you didn't," Hank said. "But I thought one of your guests might have left one behind. Why don't you check the Lost And Found?"

Talbot wasn't going to put out that much effort without a little priming, though. "What do you want an iron for, anyway, Metcalf? You seem to like the casual look just as much as I do."

"I don't like it, but living out of trash bags doesn't give me much choice," Hank muttered between his teeth.

"Watch it, Metcalf. The Carriage may not be much, but it's mine. Besides, I've seen some that was a whole lot worse and a whole lot more expensive."

"I wasn't referring to—" Hank broke off, not wanting to explain in detail. "Just see if you got an iron, Talbot."

"Might as well, I guess, since you already got me up. Probably never be able to get back to sleep now." Talbot continued complaining as he pulled his Lost And Found box out from under the counter and began fumbling through its contents. "Well, I'll be darn . . ."

Hank leaned over the desktop. "What did you find?"

"Look!" Talbot grinned up at him. "A bicentennial quarter. Wonder how that got into the box? Must have fallen out of the cash drawer, I guess."

"Must have," Hank agreed. "It sure couldn't have slipped through that tight fist of yours. Damn it, is there an iron in there or not?"

"Now, Metcalf, just simmer down a little. I'm not finished looking. I . . . Hold on. What's this? Could be. Hmm. By golly, I think it is."

Hank didn't dare look over the edge this time. He was liable to strangle Talbot if the man was kidding around again. But the innkeeper set a surprisingly new steam iron on top of the counter. "Thanks, Jackson."

"No problem, man. However, there will be a slight—"

"Just add it to my tab," Hank told him, grabbing the iron before Talbot changed his mind. With any luck, he'd be able to make himself and his wedding and funeral suit presentable in time for the ten-forty-five church service.

SUSAN HADN'T BEEN looking forward to returning to her Sunday-school class. Only her pride kept her from chickening out. She wasn't going to let a bunch of busybodies get the best of her. Besides, some of those busybodies were good friends. And Morristown was still a small enough place that you didn't sacrifice good friends lightly.

In actuality, it hadn't been that bad, Susan reflected as she gathered her children after class and steered them toward the church for the morning service. In fact, the people she'd cared about had put forth extra effort to be nice today. She would have preferred that they acted normal, but it wasn't worth staying mad.

A flurry of whispers interrupted her thoughts as they reached the sanctuary entrance. "What's wrong, you two?"

"Nothing, Mother," Kim answered quickly. "We've just decided we'd rather sit downstairs today."

"But your friends always sit in the balcony," Susan protested as Kim grabbed her hand and started heading down the red carpet that divided the main level of the church in two. "Don't you want to be with them?"

"That's only for kids," Kim announced without pausing. "Jake and I are too old for that now."

"Kim, honey, slow down," Susan begged her daughter as they continued down the aisle. "Jake, is this okay with you?" she asked the boy lagging behind them.

Her son merely shrugged.

"Kim, there are plenty of seats back here." Susan tried again to halt her daughter. "Let's sit down."

"Just a little farther," the girl promised. "Here, this is a good row. You slide in first, Mom. I want to sit next to Jake."

"You *want* to sit next to your brother? Kim, are you feeling okay?"

"Yes, Mother. No, don't sit there," Kim begged as Susan started to tuck in her skirt. "The view is much better from the center."

Without even being given the chance to turn around, Susan found herself being herded on down the bench until she felt a set of hard thighs hit the backs of her knees.

"I'm so sorry," Susan began as she turned to apologize to the poor soul she'd almost tripped over. "I didn't—Hank?"

"No harm done, Snookums," her husband assured as he scooted over two inches. Grasping her elbow, he wedged Susan into the narrow space left between Kim and himself. "There's plenty of room. See?" Then he leaned forward and across her lap to check on Kim and Jake. "You two doing okay down there?"

"Just fine, Dad." Kim grinned back at him.

Satisfied, Hank settled back in his seat as if this had always been their family pew.

"What are you doing here? You never go to church."

"Never say never in this house," Hank reminded his wife. "This is the place where anything's possible. Besides, I'm just following your suggestion and trying to set a good example for the kids."

Susan swung her gaze around to her children, who quickly snapped their eyes toward the pulpit and tried to pretend that's where they'd been looking the whole time. Then she looked around the room and caught several spies snapping their eyes toward the pulpit just a second too late.

"That's fine," she finally whispered, "but I'm afraid you've also created more unwanted publicity for us."

Hank took a look around them and found a few people looking back with undisguised curiosity. "So what—" he dismissed the stares "—there's nothing exciting about a family attending church together."

"Your being in church for something other than a wedding or a funeral is enough to keep the gossips going for a week," Susan explained in a tired voice. "Sitting next to your estranged spouse guarantees we'll be a hot topic for at least a month."

"All right, all right. I'll move to another pew, then."

Susan clamped her fingers around one of his rock-hard thighs. "Don't you dare. Any move you make now will only make the situation worse. Just stay put."

"Yes, Snookums."

Hank covered her hand with his, sliding his hand up a little.

Susan's eyes widened in surprise as she snatched her hand back into the safety of her own lap. "For heaven's sake, Hank. Remember where you're at."

"I thought this was the ideal place to get reacquainted in the biblical sense."

"That's not funny."

"Sorry, I'll behave."

"Just be quiet. That should help."

It was the longest service in Susan's memory. Each hymn had four verses. The reverend seemed determined to cover the whole New Testament in one sermon. And when the collection plate came by, it seemed that everyone had either lost their contribution in the bottom of their purse or shoved it into the wrong pocket.

Finally, Reverend Holland began the standard closing. "Refreshments will be served in Fellowship Hall, so don't everyone hurry home. But before we go quench our thirst, let's invite our guests to become part of our family. If there is anyone visiting who'd like to join our congregation, please come forward as we all exchange blessings and greetings."

When Susan turned to shake hands with the person behind her, as was the custom, she found the whole congregation was waiting to see if Hank would be making the trip down the aisle.

"Go ahead, Hank." Linda Bowen leaned forward from the next pew to give her encouragement. "Make it official."

"Yes, please," Karen Randall agreed. "If you join, maybe we'll be able to convince Mike and Junior to start coming."

Hank turned around slowly to smile at the two women. "No offense, ladies. But in that case, I think the members might prefer that I stayed a visitor."

"Amen!" shouted a man from two rows back. As the whole section began to laugh, the congregation broke up and filed out the exits.

"Come on, kids. Let's go," Susan urged her children as several of Hank's clients came over to speak with him.

"But shouldn't we wait for Dad?" Kim asked.

"It's okay, pumpkin. You go ahead," said Hank, turning away from his friends for a moment and showing Susan that her escape attempt hadn't gone unnoticed. "I'll be home for dinner, which should be ready when, Suz? Five? Six?"

Susan reminded herself of their location and answered, saccharine sweet, "Whenever you bring it, *dear.*"

Hank merely gave his grinning cronies a very masculine shrug, saying, "It's tough. But you can't live without them, boys. Trust me."

A chorus of male laughter was still ringing in Susan's ears as she ushered her kids into the car for the drive home. It wasn't fair. It just wasn't fair. Everyone seemed to be jumping over to Hank's side. She was beginning to understand why crime victims felt they were punished more than the guilty party.

As if to prove the point, Kim began to plead her father's case. "It's great, isn't it? Daddy sitting in church with us. And with him eating dinner at the house tonight, it'll be almost like he's home again. Maybe we can actually celebrate Christmas like a normal family."

Susan could see the fantasy Kim was weaving. "Honey, don't get your hopes up. Christmas is still two weeks away. Anything could happen in that time. Besides, Thanksgiving wasn't so bad, was it? You and Jake did get to eat two dinners."

"Yeah, and they were both miserable," her daughter informed her. "Jake and I would much rather celebrate

Christmas once with our parents together. Besides, you can't let Dad spend Christmas in that crummy motel. Nobody deserves that."

She had a point there, Susan admitted. She wouldn't make a dog spend Christmas at the Carriage Motel. "How do you feel about it, Jake?" Susan asked her son, who'd been sitting quietly in the back seat. "Do you want your dad to spend Christmas at home?"

"I don't know. I guess so," came his glum reply. "Whatever you want, Mom."

"It would just be for the day," Susan warned her daughter. "I don't want you to get the idea that Dad spending Christmas at the house meant anything more."

"But you never know," Kim protested. "Anything could happen. You might even want him back after a couple of days."

"A couple of days?"

"Sure," Kim explained. "He'd have to spend Christmas Eve at the house, too. Someone has to help you put our stuff together."

"What happened to Santa and his elves? Did they go on strike?"

"Give it a rest, Mom," Jake spoke up voluntarily this time. "We're way too old for that stuff."

Susan sighed. "So much for the magic of Christmas. I trust you haven't outgrown receiving gifts, though?"

"No way," the kids answered as one.

Susan sighed. "No, of course not." In fact, the items on their wish list were getting bigger and more expensive. She thought about the basketball hoop being stored at her parents' farm. Kim had been right about one thing: Susan was going to need a hand getting their presents put together. Very few of this year's gifts were going to fit in neatly wrapped boxes under the tree.

Kim barely let Hank get in the door that evening before she began issuing the Christmas invitation. Hank shot a wary glance at her mother. "Is this okay with you, Susan?"

His wife nodded reluctantly. "Yes. Kim and Jake would both like you to spend Christmas Eve and Christmas Day here at the house. I think we could maintain a truce for at least that long, don't you?"

"No problem." Hank grinned. Things were working out even better than he'd planned.

His growing confidence was visible. Susan watched it expand throughout dinner, and wasted no time in squashing it as soon as the children had departed for their youth-group meeting.

"Don't get any ideas, Hank. Nothing has changed. I think it's important that the children know they can count on both of us even though we're not together anymore. Besides, it was your idea to get that blasted basketball hoop. You're the one that's going to have to put it up."

"No problem," Hank agreed, his air of confidence not diminished one whit. "I was thinking about doing a little work on the basement, too. Since you're giving Jake that old developing equipment from the newspaper, we might as well give him an official darkroom to go with it. If it's okay with you, I'll come in next week while they're still at school and put in shelves and worktables for him."

The thought of Hank being back in the house for any length of time bothered Susan, but she had no grounds for objecting. Legally, it was still his house, too. "I guess it's all right," she said.

Determined to dispel the spirit of the family unit before it got too comfortable, Susan reached for the separation agreement and picked a topic bound to cause controversy.

"Now, about custody, since 'tis the season, we might as well go ahead and set the terms for future holidays. We can either agree to take the kids for alternate occasions, or agree to split time on the given day."

"What's wrong with the way we're doing it this year?" Hank suggested. "Let's just agree to set aside our disagreements for special occasions and let the kids enjoy having two parents."

Susan tossed her head. "No, Hank. I'm doing it this year to help them make the transition. But by next year, you and I should both have developed our own separate lives. I don't think that sort of arrangement would be agreeable to either of us, then."

"What do you mean, 'our own separate lives'?" Hank asked—although he knew exactly what she was hinting at. "Are you seeing someone I don't know about?"

"No!" The denial was automatic. "But the fact is that most divorced people do remarry. Quite soon, as a matter of fact."

"Is that why you're pushing for a divorce now? You want to get out and find a replacement?"

"We agreed that a divorce was the only answer."

"No, we didn't."

"Hank—"

"You decided it all by yourself," Hank reminded her. "You're the one who went to see Lara. You're the one who wrote that stupid draft. I've never agreed to any of it."

"But don't you agree that it's the only solution?" Susan demanded.

"Hell, no!" Hank shouted. "I think getting a divorce is the worst thing for everybody. And I think if you'll give yourself time, you'll see that, too."

"The only thing left to think about are details, Hank. Who gets what, and so on. That's what this meeting's for."

"But if neither of us is seeing someone else, what's the hurry? Taking a little time to reconsider can't hurt anything. Listen," he suggested, forestalling her arguments, "I'll make a deal with you. You agree to a truce from now till after Christmas. I mean, not one mention of the *D* word. If you still want a divorce after that, I promise I'll sign your agreement. Fair enough?"

Susan stared across the table at Hank, wishing she had a clue as to what he was really thinking. She used to know this man. Inside and out. But every encounter with him lately had only reinforced the feeling that she was dealing with a stranger. When had they lost contact with each other?

"Well?" he prompted, still waiting for an answer.

What choice did she have, really? Susan wondered. If she said no, he'd just refuse to accept everything she had written out. Maybe if she humored him for a couple of weeks, he'd see that there was no going back. At least the kids would have one last Christmas to remember.

"All right," she accepted at last. "A truce, until the day after Christmas."

Hank grinned, his confidence more evident than ever. "You won't regret it, Snookums."

Susan cringed at the familiar pet name. "I wish you'd stop calling me that."

"What?" Hank looked truly perplexed. "Snookums? But I've always called you that."

"And I've never liked it. My sister used to have a dog named Snookums."

"I bet it was a cute, fuzzy little dog filled with curiosity."

"As a matter of fact, it was a bad-tempered little bitch prone to biting men. It bit you once, remember?"

Hank winced as he felt a faint twinge at his ankle. "That was Snookums?"

"Umm-hmm."

"So, how do you feel about Poopsie?"

8

SUSAN KNEW AGREEING to the truce was a big mistake. From the minute she'd said yes, Hank began trying to worm his way back into the house.

She didn't know how he'd managed to get the time off from the Farmer's Seed & Supplies, but she knew he was spending entirely too much time in his former home. He arrived before breakfast and stayed for dinner, working on the basement while the kids were gone. When the family came home, Hank hung around helping Jake with his science experiment, discussing training strategies with Kim, and making a general nuisance of himself where his wife was concerned.

Susan tried to counter his actions by spending more and more time at the office, but apparently the truce knew no boundaries. First, Hank came by to see the *Gazette*'s darkroom, so he'd have an idea what he was building. When she started working later to avoid him, he simply brought dinner to her. Her whole staff were buzzing about it, and Susan was tired of denying their relationship.

She was almost grateful when Christmas Eve came. Though it meant spending the entire evening in Hank's company, it also signified that the truce was nearing an end. Besides, the kids would be there.

Susan had been counting on safety in numbers when she'd agreed to invite Hank. Unfortunately, the kids had no sooner finished drying the dinner dishes on Christmas Eve than Kim was dragging Jake off to go street caroling with friends.

Hank turned to his wife with a devilish, "Alone at last" smile glinting off his strong white teeth.

"Well, I guess we could work on the agreement some more," Susan tried desperately. She hurried to her to pigeonhole desk to retrieve her edition of the separation document. "Ahh, here it is. Now, which clause would you like to—"

Hank calmly took the document out of her hands and shoved it back in its place. "No way. Not on Christmas Eve. The truce is still on. No mention of the *D* word."

He was standing much too close. To her surprise and sorrow, Susan could feel her breasts begin to swell, her nipples hardening in eager anticipation. Much lower, an unbearable emptiness craved fulfillment. She wheeled away from him, spinning into the center of the room where she hoped the air was cooler, the atmosphere less charged. "Well, I guess I'd better finish wrapping those presents, then."

Hank snuck up behind her, closing his hands around her arms, drawing her back against his chest. "There'll be time for that later, when the kids are asleep."

"They're not so little anymore. Kim and Jake aren't going to be so easily persuaded to be tucked in this year."

Hank circled his arms around her. "How about you? How easy would it be to talk you into bed?"

Susan could feel her knees starting to tremble. Determined not to succumb to her baser instincts, she locked them into a stiff, straight-legged stance. "Actually, I am a little tired. A nap isn't a bad idea. Just let yourself out, Hank. I'll see you in the morning."

Hank lifted his hands to her shoulders and gently turned her around to face him. "That's not what I had in mind."

"Well, that's all I have in mind," Susan lied bravely.

"Mom, are you okay?"

Jake was standing in the threshold watching them anxiously. "Let her go," he ordered his father. "Leave her alone."

Susan took advantage of Hank's astonishment and stepped easily out of his embrace. "It's okay, Jake. Everything's all right." She hurried to her son's side, throwing her arms around her life preserver with gratitude. "What brought you back here? Did you forget something?"

"My hat," he answered distractedly. "I forgot my hat." Reluctantly he tore his angry glare away from his father's face. "Are you sure everything's all right, Mom? I'll stay here if you want me to."

"Nonsense!" Susan found it easy to dismiss her near catastrophe now that she had the width of the room between Hank and herself. She pulled Jake's hat off the hook behind the door and tugged it down over his ears. "You go out and have fun. I'm just fine."

Closing the door behind him, she turned and rested her back against the cool wood panel. One quick glance at a dazed Hank convinced her that she wasn't going to have to worry about fending off his advances for the rest of the evening.

"I don't understand," Hank said. "What got into him? He thought I was trying to hurt you."

Susan shrugged. "Jake's just feeling a little overly protective. It's perfectly natural. After all, he's been the man of the house since you left."

"But I thought he and I were getting closer. Damn it, Susan, I've really been trying to become his friend."

"Is that what this science project's been all about? And the darkroom? You're trying to make Jake your bosom buddy?"

"I'm just trying to establish a normal father-son relationship."

"Why, Hank? So you can turn him against me, too? So you can get custody of both Kim and Jake? Is that what this is all about?"

"Turn him against you?" Hank seemed stunned by the accusation. "Custody? Hell, woman! What kind of a SOB do you think I am?" He thundered across the room, eliminating her margin of safety.

Susan felt the doorknob pressing into her back as he braced his hands against the door and leaned over her. "Why, then, Hank? You never spent this much time with Jake before."

"That's precisely why I'm trying to make up for lost time now," he said. "I know I haven't been the best father to Jake. I'm trying to change that before it's too late. Surely you can understand that. Haven't you been trying to do the same thing with Kim?"

Susan flushed guiltily. "Kim thinks I care more about my career than I care about her. I've just been trying to show her that it isn't true."

"See. You're doing the same thing I am. I didn't accuse you of having ulterior motives, though." Hank pushed himself away from the door, turning away from his wife. "You really don't think much of me anymore, do you?"

"I'm sorry, Hank." Susan tentatively reached out a hand to touch his shoulder. "It seems like my whole world has been falling apart lately. I'm terrified that I might lose the children, too."

"You think I'm not scared?" Hank spun around, catching her hand in his before she could take it back. "Try spending months all alone in that fleabag motel and see how scared you get. You've no idea how much I miss those kids, this house. You."

Susan felt her uncertainties rushing back again. "I know it must be difficult for you, but I'm sure everything will be much better after you get a place of your own."

"A place of my own? Listen to what I'm saying, Susan. It's not a house I'm missing. It's my family. It's you."

Hank gave her arm a tug, pulling her closer, pressing her possessively against his chest. As his mouth closed on hers, Susan forgot about using her arms as a wedge to keep their bodies separate and looped them over his broad shoulders, letting her fingers nest in his ink-black hair.

Hank parted her lips and thrust his tongue inside to explore the once familiar territory. His hands began to travel, sliding up and down Susan's smooth, lean form. "Lord, I've missed you," he whispered huskily. "Can't you see that, Susan?" He cupped his palms around the curves of her buttocks and pulled her softness up hard against him. "Can't you feel how much I want you?"

Susan trembled with an almost-uncontrollable need. She wanted nothing more at that moment than to give in, to welcome him back into her bed. The sound of feet stomping on the doormat outside was the only thing that saved her. She wrenched herself out of Hank's grasp just as the door opened to admit their offspring once more.

"You weren't gone long." Her voice was unusually high and loud.

"It was too cold to stay out any longer. Besides, the other kids all went home." Jake darted sharp, penetrating looks from one parent to the other. "Is everything okay, Mom?"

"Yes, yes. I told you I'd be fine," Susan assured him quickly, trying to sound normal again.

"Of course, she is. Why shouldn't she be?" Kim jostled her brother with a well-aimed elbow. "I told you we didn't have to rush home."

Susan caught the pained expression that flickered across Hank's face and swiftly tried to change the focus of attention. "I'm glad you're back, anyway. We've got a million things to do."

More like a billion, it seemed to Hank. His wife kept him busy with one chore after the other all evening and through Christmas Day. And whenever Susan faltered in coming up with yet another task, Jake conveniently intervened and demanded her attention.

All too soon, Christmas was over. The truce had ended.

9

HANK CAUGHT Susan's hand as they called one last good-night and "Merry Christmas" up the stairs to Kim and Jake. Then he pulled his wife out onto the front porch.

"Hank, what do you think you're doing?"

"Shh," he hushed her. "You'll have Jake coming after me with a shotgun if you keep yelling like that."

"I'm not sure that's such a bad idea," she said, lowering her voice nevertheless. "What did you drag me out here for?"

"To talk about Jake, actually. You've got to help me, Susan. The situation between him and me is getting worse instead of better. You and Kim seem to have patched the quilt. How did you do it? How did you get her to stop looking at you like you were the enemy?"

Susan quit trying to wrestle her arm out of his grip. "I don't know. I've been spending more time with her. It's a lot easier now that she's coming out of the tomboy stage a little. She and I are beginning to have more things in common—clothes, hair, makeup, men—the usual women things."

"Fat lot of good that'll do me."

"Hold on, that's just what we started with. Kim and I have discovered a lot of things we can talk about. Like the environment. Kim and I are both very concerned about that. She's even helping me work out a plan to recycle old newspapers. I'm sure you and Jake could find something in common. Like the darkroom, for instance. He loved that." Susan snapped her fingers. "Say, there's an idea right there. Why don't you take up photography?"

But Hank shook his head. "No. I already thought of that, but it's not my sort of thing. Surely Jake is interested in something besides taking pictures, though."

"Drawing, painting, writing."

Hank shook his head again. "Let's forget the arts-and-crafts stuff. Doesn't he like any sports?"

"Not that I can think of." Susan leaned against the porch railing and mentally ran through a list of her son's interests. "Sorry, Hank. About the only thing else Jake likes to do is read." She laughed when she saw her husband's grimace. "Come on. It's not that bad. You've got a library card. All you would have to do is use it."

"I think I'm a little old for the Hardy boys."

"So's Jake. He finished reading those three or four years ago. He's into science fiction now."

"Science fiction?"

"You know. Space travel, time warps, other worlds. Here, I'll show you." Susan led Hank to the back of the station wagon and hauled a grocery sack filled with paperbacks out of the cargo section. "I've been meaning to drop these off at the library for the literacy book sale. Why don't you take a look at them? Who knows, you might like them. You used to be really interested in astronomy, remember?"

"I remember."

Susan looked up at him, surprised by the huskiness of his voice. She saw the smoldering look in his eyes and hastily glanced away. Stupid, stupid, stupid. How could she have set herself up like that?

Hank stroked one finger gently down her cheek. "I remember driving out on Rabbit Road, way past town, out where the only lights were the moon and the stars. I remember lying down with you on that quilt your grandmother made. I remember showing you the constellations. I remember touching them when we—"

"That's enough, Hank."

"Not for me it isn't. I want to touch them again, Susan. With you."

"Stop it. That's all in the past."

Hank tried to take away the sack she clutched between them, but Susan refused to let go. "I mean it, Hank. The only thing we're discussing is a divorce. I don't need any trips down memory lane."

"I think you do," Hank argued. "I think if you remembered how good it used to be with us, you'd forget about all this nonsense. Damn it, Susan. I want to come home!"

Susan swung her head violently back and forth. "No, Hank. Don't confuse the issue now. Everything's almost settled."

"Nothing's settled!" he objected vehemently. "Hell, Susan, we haven't even come close to reaching a settlement agreement. Don't you think it's because neither of us really wants one?"

"No. I think it's because you're so pigheaded you won't listen to reason. But it doesn't matter now. The truce is over. You said you'd sign the agreement, Hank. There's nothing left to argue about."

Hank glanced at his watch. Eleven o'clock. "I've still got one more hour coming. Give me a chance, Snookums. Let me show you how good it could be if you'd just let me come home."

He pressed his lips against hers as she opened her mouth to protest, stealing what he had hoped she would give him freely. With the heavy sack of books filling her arms, Susan was helpless against his invasion. And as the kiss dragged on, she lost all inclination to struggle.

When Hank drew back at last, they were both gasping for air. "There's still something there, Snookums." He rescued the sack of books before her limp arms completely lost their hold, setting the bag on the ground. "If you'll at least be honest with yourself, you'll know there's still something there."

"It doesn't matter," Susan whispered huskily.

"It has to," her husband insisted. "look, I'm not suggesting that I move back home tonight. I know you're not ready for that. But just listen to me."

Susan hesitated, then nodded slowly. "Go ahead."

"I want us to continue the negotiations. If we can talk—"

"But you said you'd sign the agreement as is, if I agreed to the truce," Susan reminded him. "You promised."

"I'm not talking about the separation agreement, Suz."

"But then, what do you want to negotiate?"

"A reconciliation. I'm serious," he told her when she gasped. "I want to discuss your terms for my moving back home."

"There are no terms, Hank. It's simply out of the question."

"Why? Susan, whether you believe me or not, there has to be some way we can work things out. I can't believe you won't give me a chance to make things up."

"It's not that simple, Hank. Too much has happened. Things between us have changed. We've changed."

"Maybe that's what we need to talk about, then," Hank suggested. "Just think about it over the week. You can give me your answer next Sunday. I'll come for dinner just as if we were going to discuss the separation agreement. The kids won't even have to know the difference. That way if things don't work out . . ."

"They won't get their hopes up," she finished for him. "At least we can agree on that much."

Susan sighed heavily. She couldn't believe she was even considering it, but she was. After all, what harm could it do to talk about it? Maybe she'd at least learn how their marriage had gotten so far off course.

"All right. I'll think about it until Sunday."

"You won't regret it, Snookums. I promise."

Hank leaned forward to steal another swift kiss, then grabbed his sack of books and walked backward to his truck, grinning at her confidently the whole way. Susan was still shaking her head as he drove down the block. "I know one thing," she muttered to herself as she headed inside. "The first item is going to be No More Snookums!"

Unfortunately, she couldn't decide what the second item should be. Every time she tried to list her terms on a sheet of paper, she ended up crumpling the piece into a tight wad and adding it to the growing pile of trash. Whichever way Susan added it up, she couldn't make it equal a reconciliation.

The week fled by and all too soon it was Sunday. Hank appeared in church again to share her hymnal, then wished his family goodbye until dinner. He arrived at the house at six o'clock, taking his place at the head of the table.

He shared small talk with Kim, trying to draw Jake into the conversation and all the while sneaking sideways peeks at his wife in an attempt to forecast the weather at the opposite end of the table. Cold front? A warming trend? It was impossible to tell.

"Have you thought about what I asked?" Hank began awkwardly as soon as the door closed behind Jake and Kim. "Do you have your terms prepared?"

"No." Susan shook her head. "I couldn't find anything to put in writing. Hank, I'm afraid it's just not going to work."

He clenched and unclenched his fists, his mouth tightening with tension. "You can't dismiss it that easily, Susan. I don't expect this to be easy, but it can't be impossible."

"I don't even know where to start," Susan told him. "I don't know where we went wrong in the first place. Maybe if you could explain that, I would know where to start fixing things."

Hank rubbed his head as if it ached. "I've already told you how it happened, Susan. I was mad. I had too much to drink when I was in a sour mood. Sandra was in the wrong place at the wrong time. It was just one big mistake."

"I think it was more than that." Susan gazed at him from across the table, searching his lean, dark face for more clues. "You've been hanging out at the Jube more and more over the past two years. Ever since I bought the *Gazette*. You've been drinking more and yelling more. You've become impossible to talk to.

"You haven't been happy in a long time," she continued. "That's why you were at the Jube that night. I think that's why you went home with Sandra."

Hank's eyes stared into hers, obsidian-black circles impossible for her to read. "It's the truth," Susan whispered sadly, when he failed to protest. "And I wasn't any happier than you were. It's taken the past few months of living alone to make me appreciate how unhappy I was."

Her husband jerked as if he'd been physically wounded. His worst fears were being confirmed.

"Don't get me wrong." Susan gently reached out and covered one of his large, clenched fists with her fingers. "I have missed you, Hank. There have been nights when I ached for you so bad I didn't think I'd live till morning."

Hank opened his hand, ready to grasp hers and hang on for all he was worth. But Susan slid out of his warm grasp, withdrawing any hints of hope.

"But I survived, Hank. And, after a while, I began to realize there are a lot of things I don't miss at all." She closed her eyes and flexed her shoulders as if she was still feeling the relief of a huge weight being taken off her shoulders.

"I don't miss fighting over the *Gazette* every time I work late. I don't miss arguing over the profits I have to put back into the newspaper. I don't miss being typecast as a neglectful wife and mother just because I love my work."

"I've never accused you of being a bad mother!" Hank sputtered at last.

"Just a bad wife, then," Susan said. "That makes me feel much better."

Her husband cursed his clumsy tongue. "Damn it, woman. You know that's not what I meant."

"Isn't it? We both know you've done more than your fair share around the house over the past couple of years. You always took great pains to make sure I knew just how much was left for you to do every time I worked late."

"I wasn't trying to criticize you," Hank protested. "I only wanted to be given credit for what I did."

"Well, I'm tired of keeping score of who does what and who owes who."

"Then don't." Hank caught her fingers again, squeezing them tightly. "I'll support your work from now on. I promise. Hell, I'll do all the cooking and cleaning if that's what it takes. Fair enough?"

"No, it's not." Susan tugged her hand free as she stood and backed away. "I'm not going to let you make a martyr of yourself again, Hank. That would just make me the Judas and, quite frankly, it's not worth the price. Even if you could be the perfect modern husband, it wouldn't be worth the never-ending guilt trip."

Hank stared at the chair she had vacated. "You've lost me. First you tell me I have to be more supportive, then you say that my support makes you feel guilty. What do you want from me, Susan?"

"I want—" She hesitated, searching for the right words. "I want a marriage where nobody tries to keep tabs. Where both parties give what they can and take what they need without leaving each other feeling shortchanged.

"But more than anything else, Hank—" Susan paused, taking a deep breath. This was the hardest part. "More than anything else, I want to be able to trust you again. I want to be able to believe in our happiness without being afraid I'm kidding myself."

"I give you my word," Hank swore.

"I had your word before, your wedding vow. It didn't prevent something from happening. Words are easy, Hank. They're no guarantee against the future."

"But if we could settle everything else, then maybe the trust would be there," Hank suggested. "Susan, we can set it all down in black and white if that's what it takes. Who's responsible for what. Whose turn it is to cook or clean or whatever. There will be no doubts about what we expect from each other. No surprises for either of us."

"I don't know." Susan looked doubtful. "Maybe the household chores can be divided up on paper, but I still don't see a way around the most important problem. You can't negotiate trust, Hank. It's either there or it's not."

"At least give it a chance," her husband pleaded, looking more humble than Susan had ever seen him. "Let's start with things we can negotiate and go from there."

When Susan hesitated, visibly wavering between one decision and the other, Hank pushed on, desperately trying to tilt the balance in his favor. "What should we discuss first? The household chores, finances—"

"The kids," Susan interrupted. "Kim and Jake have to come first."

Hank shook his head. "But if we stay together, there's no custody issue."

"No, but we still have our responsibilities as parents," Susan reminded him. "We've both been guilty of letting our personal problems get in the way of parenting. Kim and Jake deserve more. Whether we reconcile or divorce."

"You're right," Hank admitted. "But what do you have in mind?"

Susan paced slowly. "I think we need to figure out some sort of plan where we can each spend time with each child. I don't want to lose what ground I've gained with Kim, and you've already admitted you need help getting through to Jake."

"Agreed." He nodded. "And we need to do more things as a family."

"Right," Susan said. "All we have to do is figure out where we're going to get the time."

"We'll make the time," Hank told her. "Like you said, the kids have to come first. Before the *Gazette*, or," he added quickly, "the Farmer's Seed and Supplies."

She was saved from a response by a quick glance at the clock. "I think we'd better call it quits for tonight. The kids will be home soon."

"Same time, next week?"

Susan hesitated. "I'm still not sure this is going to work, Hank. I'm not promising anything."

"I understand," he assured her. "But we've got nothing to lose by trying." *Unless it doesn't work*, he finished silently.

"Then same time, next week," Susan said.

THE NEXT SUNDAY they finished "Children" and started on "Household Chores." Then they tackled "Finances," and finally, "Careers."

"Face it, Susan," Hank said six weeks later as the clock indicated the hour for negotiations was nearing its end. "There are some things we're going to have to agree to disagree on. I still think you're spending too much time at work. However," he tacked on, preempting her arguments, "there are some things I'm prepared to live with."

"And I guess I'm supposed to live with the fact that you're driving a stick of dynamite."

"It's called compromise," Hank informed her. "I think we're getting pretty good at it. We've agreed that you'll take over Kim's Cadette troop and I'll try to get Jake to enlist in the Boy Scouts with me. Whoever gets home first has to start dinner. Tuesday nights the whole family will clean house—chores to be determined by lottery method. Thursday nights, family recreation to be determined by a majority vote. There's only one major decision left."

"Which is?"

"When can I come home?"

Susan sighed. "Hank..."

"Okay," he said. "Maybe it's not the only decision left, but it's the most important. Anything else, we can work out. The past few weeks have proven that."

His wife shook her head. "I just don't know."

"Then what will it take to convince you?"

"I don't know!" Susan paced restlessly, as had become her habit during their weekly meetings. The closer she and Hank came to settling their differences, the more nervous she became. Everything else aside, did she want her husband back? Did she dare trust him enough to take him back?

"I need more time, Hank."

"How much?"

"I don't know. You can't set a deadline for something like this."

"But don't you think the sooner we take this family out of limbo and put it back together, the better?"

"Maybe," Susan answered, getting more and more flustered. "I don't know." She heard a car door slam outside. Kim and Jake were back. She'd been saved for another week. "The kids are here, Hank. We'll talk about it next Sunday, okay?"

"Friday," he corrected.

"What?"

"Friday. It's Valentine's Day, remember? The youth group is having a party and sleep-over at the church. We'll have all night to discuss our reconciliation." *And to celebrate.*

"All night?" Susan repeated weakly.

"That's right, Snookums. All night."

10

"FIFTY-FIVE, FIFTY, forty-five, forty..." Susan began counting with Hank's first knock and forced herself to finish the countdown before opening the door. She was going to need all the composure she could muster to get through this evening.

Thank heavens, she had gone to see Lara.

As the morning light had begun to shine through the bedroom window that Valentine's Day, Susan still hadn't come up with any clear answers, but she had finally narrowed it down to what seemed the simplest solution. After all, if she took Hank back and it didn't work out, they could always get divorced later.

She tried to explain that to Lara Jamison that afternoon, hoping the attorney would agree with her decision. She should have known better. Lara had seen the indecision clearly written on her client's face and wisely suggested another option. Susan had immediately sensed that this new alternative was the right one.

Now, if she could just get Hank to listen to reason.

"I WAS BEGINNING to think you'd forgotten I was coming," Hank groused when she finally answered the door. Then his gaze traveled slowly from her carefully styled hair to the little black slip-dress. "Looks like I was worrying over nothing." His voice thickened huskily, its warmth raising a pinkish glow in her cheeks. "You look great, Snookums."

She had worn a hole in her bedroom carpet trying to decide what to wear. Afraid of giving Hank a false impression, she had almost opted for her usual wardrobe of jeans with a sweater or sweatshirt. At the last minute, she had changed her mind. Hank wouldn't be staying long after she made her announcement. The little black dress would give him something to think about after he had time to calm down.

"I guess we were of like mind, for once," she said with a glance at the Sunday suit he had on.

"In that case, I'm sure we will have a lot to celebrate." Hank swooped down to claim her mouth possessively. When he drew back, a floral fragrance replaced the spicy smell of his after-shave and Susan felt the soft, velvety caress of rose petals against her skin. "Happy Valentine's Day."

"Oh, Hank! They're beautiful!" Stunned and delighted, she took the bouquet he offered. "A dozen roses! I can't believe it." She touched her nose to a fragile blood-red bloom. "No one's ever brought me roses before."

"I know." Hank bowed his head with guilt.

"Oh, no. I wasn't criticizing," Susan hurried to assure him. "I never expected any. Honest. It would have been silly to have spent money on roses when we could barely make ends meet. I guess it's still silly, for that matter, but I do love them." *Shut up and kiss him, stupid.* Rising up on her toes, she did just that. "Thank you, Hank."

"You're welcome." He cupped his hands around her elbows and held her in place while he returned the salute. Gently, he let her ease back down, but he didn't let her go. "So, tell me, Susan. Should I get the bags out of the truck?"

"I, uh, think I'd better go put these in water." Susan spun out of his arms and hurried to the kitchen, with Hank following on her heels.

"You're stalling," he accused as he lounged against a countertop and watched her scrounge for a container.

Guilty as charged, she finished arranging the roses in a makeshift vase, then placed them in the center of the table set for two. "Why don't we save the discussion until after dinner?"

"What's to discuss? The answer is either yes or no."

"Not necessarily."

His eyes narrowed in suspicion. "What is that supposed to mean?"

"I really think we should save this for later. I bought a couple of steaks for dinner. Why don't you put them on the grill while I get everything else ready?"

"Why don't you just answer my question?"

Susan gave up. It was obvious that the only thing Hank intended to grill was his wife. "All right. Let's go in the living room and talk."

With a sudden, chilling premonition, Hank knew that he wasn't going to like the answer. "I'd rather go upstairs to our bedroom."

"I don't recall us doing much talking there."

"Precisely."

Susan's flush was small comfort as he followed her into the living room. Any brief trace of satisfaction vanished completely when she regally claimed the wing chair that had once been known as "Dad's chair." Hank frowned at this subtle maneuver, his displeasure becoming more pronounced as he sank into the soft, fluffy depths of the club chair opposite.

"All right," he said when he had straightened up as much as he could. "Tell me what you meant by that comment back in the kitchen. The way I see it, the answer only requires a simple yes or no."

"That all depends on the question."

Hank waited two minutes for her to elaborate before realizing that she was waiting for him to reissue the question. It was definitely an unfair situation as far as he was concerned. Nevertheless, he cleared his throat and made a valiant effort. "Do you or do you not want us to get back together?"

"Yes."

Her quick, affirmative response took him off guard and he almost jumped to his feet with joy. Fortunately, the damned fluffy chair saved him from embarrassing himself. Its reluctance to free him allowed time for the full implications of Susan's answer to sink in. Hank surrendered to the chair again.

"Yes, you do want me back, or yes, you do not?"

"That about sums it up."

"Maybe I should rephrase the question." Hank cleared his throat and tried again. "Do you still love me?"

Susan hesitated this time. "Yes."

The answer was so softly spoken, Hank was afraid he hadn't heard correctly. "Say that again."

Her face scrunched up as if she had been asked to swallow something distasteful. "Yes."

Hank sighed with relief. "Then you do want me back."

"Not necessarily."

"Damn it, Susan. Cut that out. How am I supposed to figure out what you want from those kinds of answers?"

"I don't know." She gave up her claim to the throne and began pacing back and forth between their chairs.

"I don't know. That's the whole point, Hank. I don't know. I don't know if I can forgive what happened. I don't know if I can forget."

"But nothing did happen!" Hank fought his way out of his own seat and dogged her steps. "I told you the truth, Suz. If you don't believe me, ask Sandra. I may have gone home with her, but I didn't go through with it. I told you, you're the only woman I want."

Susan whirled around to face him, coming to an abrupt halt and almost getting herself trampled under his feet in the process. Automatically reaching up to steady Hank as he swayed off balance, her hands continued to clutch his lapels after he was stabilized.

"I may be the only one you want, but that didn't keep you from trying to find a substitute, Hank." Susan raised her voice just loud enough to drown out his protests. "And even if I'm willing to believe that your conscience saved you then, there's still no guarantee that it'll pull you out of her arms next time."

"But there won't be a next time!" At such close range, his shout was painfully on target. Hank lowered his voice contritely as he saw his wife wince. "I swear it will never happen again. You've got to believe that."

"How can I?" Susan dropped his lapels and stepped back, her eyes never leaving his. "I'm still the publisher of the *Gazette*. There are always going to be nights when I work late. I don't know if I can stand wondering if you'll be there or not when I come home."

Hank's face turned crimson. Susan could feel the air between them simmering with the heat he gave off. She braced herself for a volcanic eruption, but Hank's voice when he finally spoke was ominously mild.

"In other words, knowing I wouldn't be there because we're divorced is easier than trusting me to be there if we're still married."

Susan shifted uneasily. "I don't know about easier, but it would definitely be safer."

"And you've decided to play it safe."

"I didn't say that."

Hank cleared his throat again and squared his shoulders, standing straight and tall as if he were facing a firing squad. "Then what exactly are you saying?"

Susan's tongue flicked out to moisten her lips as she suddenly became aware of the dryness in her mouth. Her courage faltered for an instant. She lowered her lashes, retreating from his vigilant black stare and searched inward for a small shred of bravado to carry her through. Finally, refocusing her gaze on the buttons of Hank's white shirt, she continued: "I think we should give ourselves another chance—"

The buttons seemed to jump right into her face. Susan instinctively jerked back, but Hank crushed her against his chest. "Thank God. Thank God. Oh, Snookums, you won't regret it."

"Hank!" Susan spit out his lapel and tried again. "Hank, wait! Stop. You didn't let me finish."

"Never mind. You said what mattered." He crushed his mouth against hers, darting his tongue inside to restake his claim. "Sweetheart, it's been too long."

For once, Susan had to agree with him. It felt so good to hold him, to be held by him. The rest of her speech was forgotten as Hank bent down and swept one arm beneath her legs, lifting her high up against his chest. Susan uttered a token protest, but Hank merely sealed her mouth with a kiss, not releasing it until he had carried her up the stairs, lowering her onto their bed and covered her body with his.

"Shh," he hushed when she tried to speak again. "We'll talk more later. This is all that's important right now. We've got a lot of time to make up for and not enough time to do it in. I intend to make every second count. You'll see, Suz. You made the right decision. It'll be just like it used to be."

Would it? Susan panicked. Could it be the same? She had lain in this bed alone for over six months, praying that she could turn back the clock and make everything the way it used to be. But could they really do it?

She felt Hank thread his fingers through her tousled hair. She let him pull her head back so that he could have access to her mouth again. When he kissed her, she tried to kiss him back. She really tried.

But had he always nipped her lower lip like that? She didn't think so. Had another woman taught him to kiss like that? Is that the way *she* liked it?

Then his large, callused hands began to roam eagerly over her body, and Susan couldn't help but wonder if he was comparing her small breasts and bony hips to the lush, full softness of another woman. She had never had to worry about that before. They had been one-and-onlies, once. She had liked it that way. It had been safer that way.

Stop it, stop it! she told herself angrily. He wants you. He came back to you. Just forget about the rest and hold on to him this time.

She wrapped her arms around him and let her own hands renew their intimate acquaintance with his rugged frame. But his body wasn't the same, either. Hank had lost weight. The beer gut he had begun to develop over the past two years was gone. Everything had changed. Susan knew with a sudden, startling clarity that she couldn't pretend it hadn't.

HANK FELT HER withdrawal. Desperately he began to strip away their clothes, hoping her doubts would be shed with the garments restricting their joining. He had to reclaim her. He had to get her back. The caressing strokes he had bestowed were abandoned as his hands frantically squeezed her flesh, gathering her body to his, holding her captive, closing in for the final reunion.

HE HAD NEVER BEEN this rough before. Eager, yes. Demanding, yes. But not rough. Was this the way he wanted it now? Hard and fast? Wild and out of control? Susan shuddered fearfully, and her desire fled in terror. Everything had changed.

HANK DIDN'T KNOW what to do. He wanted so badly to be inside her again, to be part of her again. But Susan was tight and dry. He knew he would hurt her if he tried to enter now. He eased back, forcing himself to slow down. She was his wife, his lover. He knew her as he did no one else.

Willing himself back under control, he slid down her body, lowering his mouth to the parched valley between her legs where a warm pool of passion had once slaked his thirst. He was sure he could renew the flow of nectar if he were to conduct a thorough exploration of its source.

SUSAN FELT THE RASP of his tongue against her delicate, satiny inner folds. Images of Hank's face buried between another woman's thighs flashed against her tightly closed eyelids. She gasped at the picture and her eyes flew open, banishing the image. Hank had sworn he hadn't made love to anyone else. She had to believe him. She had to, she had to.

She couldn't.

Hysterically, she began to struggle, yanking his hair, forcing Hank to raise his head. "Susan!" Startled by his yelp of pain, Susan released the death grip she had on his thick, dark hanks of hair. Shoving her way out of his arms, she struggled to her feet and stumbled blindly across the room.

"What the hell's wrong? What did I do?" Her husband knelt in the center of the bed and stared at her in bewilderment.

Susan wrapped her arms around her chest, hugging herself protectively. "I can't. I can't do it."

"Can't do what?" Hank rolled off the mattress and approached her cautiously. "Susan, tell me what's wrong? Did I hurt you?" Gently he turned her around, pushing the mass of brown curls back from her face. "Please, sweetheart. Tell me. I can fix it. Just tell me what to do."

"You can't fix it. It's too late." Naked and vulnerable, she stood before him, her thin body racked by sobs, her words made almost indistinguishable by a stream of tears. "I can't stop thinking about you making love to someone else. I can't stop picturing you touching her the way you touch me. I can't stop wondering if you'll prefer her to me."

"No! No, Susan. Never." Instinctively, he reached out to her, ignoring her efforts to dodge his embrace. "You're the only woman I love. I could never touch someone else or want someone else. Baby, haven't you been listening to me? I can't make love to someone else. I love you."

Blind without the glasses he'd removed earlier, Susan couldn't escape. When he tried to kiss her again, she could only bury her face in the hollow of his shoulder, hiding her lips from his.

Hank thrust his hand through her hair and tugged her head back. "I'll prove it. You'll see. Just let me love you."

"No!" Susan began twisting wildly in his arms. "No. It's not the same! Nothing will ever be the same again. You don't even make love the way you used to!"

"Oh, Snookums." Hank narrowed the circle of his embrace, pinning her against his body. "I'm sorry. I'm sorry." He waited till the fight had been worn out of her, then cradled her head back against his shoulder and slowly rocked her in his arms, crooning apologies in her ear. "I'm sorry. I'm sorry. I screw up everything, don't I?"

Gradually the tension in her spine began to ebb, her tears began to ease. "That's it, Susan," he encouraged her. "That's right. Just relax. Everything will be okay. I just rushed you, that's all. Put your arms around me, sweetheart. Everything will be all right."

Hank knew that he couldn't let her go now. He couldn't let it end this way. Instinctively he knew that if he did, it would all be over for good.

As she quieted, he began to sprinkle light kisses across her shoulders and against her neck. He nibbled at the soft skin behind her ear. "Remember," he whispered. "Remember how we used to neck like this for hours, parked out on Rabbit Road? You used to get me so hard I couldn't stand it anymore and I'd have to stumble off into the woods before I exploded right there in my jeans."

One heavy hand moved down to cover her gently rounded breast, his thick fingers plucking tenderly at the nipple, mimicking the pull of a hungry mouth. "Remember what it was like when you were nursing the babies? You used to let me watch. Lord, I was jealous. I didn't want anyone to taste you but me."

"Remember," he continued, murmuring huskily as he eased her to the bed. "Remember when I discovered that you were ticklish here behind your knees?" Gently he lowered her back against the mattress and lay beside her, his hands following his words. "Remember the first time you let me touch you here, between your legs? Remember, Suz. Don't you remember?"

She let him part her thighs, lying utterly still as Hank bent to taste her again, knowing this time that his thirst would be rewarded.

"Oh, Snookums, you do remember." Hank drank his fill, then kissed his way back up to lie by her side. He took her hand and guided it down to the rigid proof of his own desire. "Remember the first time you put your hand around me? Hold me like that, Susan. Show me you remember."

Her long, slim fingers formed a tight sheath for his blatant arousal. With the edge of her thumb, Susan gently traced the pulsing vein from the damp tip to the heavy throbbing base, repeating the journey numerous times.

Her lover groaned out loud as he savored the caress and Susan thrilled at his uninhibited response. But she needed more proof. Her free hand began to glide smoothly across the flat plain of Hank's stomach, over his loins and down to the tops of his thighs.

Hank held himself still, realizing what his wife was searching for. He grinned confidently as he heard her gasp of relief, knowing that the sensitive pads of her fingertips had discovered the prickly skin covering the taut muscles of his thigh.

The gooseflesh was all Susan needed to affirm her ability to satisfy her husband. She knew the involuntary reaction was a sure sign that he was being aroused beyond the limits of his control.

Unable to wait any longer, Hank shifted their bodies. When he covered her this time, there was no hesitation on either part. Hank found the virgin path he had forged fourteen years ago slick and ready for his return. He slid inside with a smooth, fluid movement and didn't stop until he was all the way home.

SUSAN WOKE just before dawn and lay for a moment in puzzled disorientation. Could Sandra Kellogg have just been a dream, the months of separation a horrible nightmare? It seemed possible, with the familiar weight of Hank's arm lying possessively across her hips, his body providing a solid wall of support for her own.

She found herself pressing closer without even being aware of it until the movement proved just how intimately entwined they were. Hank had slipped out of her snug, damp hollow sometime during the night, but he seemed content to burrow between the soft flesh of her inner thighs.

Quite content, judging by the length, width and firmness. Susan had no doubt that when his state of arousal reached a point where it demanded attention, her husband would wake up raring to go.

Maybe Hank was right about things not changing for him. However, Susan knew that everything had changed for her. A few months ago, she would have been deciding the most delectable way to wake up her husband. Now, she was contemplating the best way to get out of bed without disturbing him. Things had definitely changed.

Moving carefully, she eased away from his body, pausing whenever Hank tightened his arms or grumbled a sleepy protest. After several stalled attempts, Susan finally managed to extricate herself. Not even daring to sigh in relief, she quietly wrapped herself in an old terry-cloth robe and tiptoed down the hall to the kids' bathroom for a shower.

She winced as the steaming-hot water cascaded down over her shoulders, but stood under the stinging spray for several minutes, letting it wash away the bittersweet scent of last night's lovemaking.

In all the years of loving Hank, she had thought they had experienced every element of marital relations. Hot sex, fun sex, sneaky sex and legal sex. Quick and hard, slow and easy. Tempting, teasing, tantalizing, tormenting. But last night had introduced a new dimension—bittersweet.

When Hank had begun the trip down memory lane, she had known exactly what he was up to with his "Remember how good it was, how sweet it was" line. She did remember. It had been good. It had been sweet. Had been…was…past tense. Now, bittersweet was the only way to describe Hank's homecoming.

Like a goodbye kiss, their lovemaking last night had been filled with memories, tinged with regrets, and haunted by the reality that something was being left behind.

Lara had been right, Susan realized now. She and Hank couldn't go back to a marriage founded by two starry-eyed teenagers. They weren't young or idealistic anymore and neither was their marriage. Their only hope was to start over again, to fall in love again—this time as two battle-scarred, disillusioned and very frightened adults.

She shut the water off with enough force to almost break off the knob and began toweling herself dry as she recalled the carefully thought-out speech she had memorized yesterday but had never gotten to give. That was a mistake she was going to remedy right now.

Marching back to the master bedroom, she shoved their door open and found Hank lying wide-awake, his eyes glued to a water stain on the ceiling.

"Why didn't you tell me the roof was leaking?" he demanded.

Susan frowned and raised her gaze to the mottled brown patch he was glaring at. "I didn't realize it was," she answered honestly. The roof had been the last thing on her mind.

"Well, it is. And if we don't fix it soon, we're going to have the whole thing falling down on our heads."

He glared at the spot so hard, Susan wouldn't have been surprised if laser beams shot out of his eyes and eliminated the flaw at that instant. Instead, she found his gaze unexpectedly trained on her.

"Is something wrong with our shower, too?"

"What?" His change of subject threw her off for a moment. "Oh, the shower. No. Nothing's wrong with it. I just didn't want to wake you."

"Why not?" Hank frowned. "If you had, we could have taken one together. Like we used too."

He couldn't have given her a better lead-in. "That was then," Susan told him. "This is now. All those memory games aren't going to get us anywhere, Hank."

It was his turn to be perplexed. "What are you talking about?"

Susan shook her head. "I think this is a discussion that should be saved for the negotiating table. Why don't you get dressed and join me downstairs, then we'll talk."

She left without waiting for an answer, leaving an astonished Hank staring after her.

WHAT THE HELL had happened? he asked himself. What had he done now? Where was the sweet, loving wife he had held in his arms last night?

Hank's hands trembled as he picked his trousers up off the floor. He pulled them on carefully, having to struggle to stay upright. Susan had really knocked him off balance this time. She couldn't have changed her mind, he told himself. It was too late. Surely Susan realized that. He was home now. *Home to stay.*

He fastened his pants, then grabbed his shirt, shrugging into it as he made his way downstairs. He could hear her banging pots and pans in the kitchen, but he didn't stray from his path.

Susan almost dropped the frying pan on her foot when she heard the front door close. Her heart began pounding furiously as she ran after her husband. Had he had second thoughts, too? Had he already decided he didn't want her anymore?

She pulled herself up short when she reached the front porch, watching him head to his truck, waiting for him to climb in and drive off into the dawn. But Hank bypassed the driver's side and headed to the back of the vehicle. Reaching over the tailgate, he leaned in and picked up one large, overstuffed green garbage bag with each hand.

"Whoa!" Susan hurried out to intercept him. "What do you think you're doing?"

Hank didn't stop walking until he and his wife were standing toe to toe, separated only by the emotionally overcharged force field that insulated one from the other. "What does it look like?" he asked with feigned innocence.

"Put them back." She issued the countermand with an authoritative voice that indicated immediate compliance was expected.

With insolent insubordination, Hank tried to step around her. Susan anticipated his move and cut him off. "I said put them back, Hank."

He closed his eyes for a second, forcing himself to check his temper. "Come on, Susan. What's the big deal? I might as well be unpacking while you make breakfast. The more settled things are before the kids get home, the better."

"That's precisely my point," Susan said, cutting him off again as he tried to dodge around her. "Nothing is settled. You and I still have a lot to talk about before Kim and Jake get here. So put the bags back. Then you can come inside."

Hank ground his teeth to hold back the expletives. "Susan—"

She stubbornly pointed to the truck.

He followed the direction of her finger with his eyes, then he looked back toward the house—their home, his castle—and dropped the bags where he stood. Grasping his wife's arm in a none-too-gentle manner, he began escorting her inside. "You want to talk? Fine. Let's start with what the hell's got into you this morning."

Susan had to practically run to keep up with his long, angry strides. She didn't complain, however, deciding she best save her wind for the storm front moving in on them. Jerking her arm out of his hand as they entered the living room, she darted for the wing chair, determined to establish an early lead in the ensuing battle. But this time Hank got there first.

With a smug smile, he lowered himself into his favorite chair, swinging his legs up onto the matching ottoman with an undeniable air of ownership. He waved his hand at the seat opposite. "Go ahead," he invited her as if she were the guest. "Have a seat. Make yourself comfortable. Then tell me what the hell your problem is."

Susan declined the offer, standing firm, her arms crossed over her chest, resisting the temptation to pace the living-room rug. Hank might read that as a sign of nervousness, of unsureness. She didn't want to give him the idea that she was anything less than certain.

"You're the problem, Hank. You think you can come home as if nothing happened."

"Not that again! Damn it, Susan. We went over this last night. Nothing *did* happen." Hank began to rise up, only to find himself being shoved back into his chair.

"I'm not talking about what you and Sandra did or didn't do, Hank, so just shut up and listen." She met Hank's shocked eyes with an unflinching stare until the big man finally sank silently back into his chair.

"Good," she praised him soothingly. "That's good. Now, as I was saying, you seem to think we can go on like nothing happened. But you're wrong, Hank. A lot has happened since you walked out that door last August. We can't just pretend that it hasn't."

"Why not?" he demanded.

"Because I've changed, Hank. And whether you're willing to admit it or not, so have you. Neither of us are the kids we were when we got married."

Hank thrust a hand through his disheveled hair. "It's last night, isn't it? I knew you weren't getting into it the way I was, but it'll come back, Susan. Just give it time. It's always been good between us."

Susan groaned. "I'm not talking about sex, Henry Jacob. I'm talking about you and me. Besides these so-called negotiations, when was the last time you and I talked about something other than the kids or the bills or whose turn it was to cook dinner? When was the last time we did something together that didn't involve Kim or Jake or one of our families? I honestly can't recall. Can you?"

Hank shrugged. He couldn't remember, either, but he didn't see what that had to do with anything. "What difference does it make?"

"It makes a big difference to me. What if we did get back together for Kim and Jake's sake now? What happens when they leave home? That day isn't very far away, Hank. If all we have going for us is the kids, what happens when the kids aren't here?"

Shivers of fear shot up his spine and Hank felt the gooseflesh pricking up on his thighs and arms as a heavy dose of adrenaline shot through his veins. It was his worst nightmare. One by one, they would all leave—Kim, Jake and then Susan—they'd go off in the world to reach their full potential, leaving poor ol' Hank behind.

"We could always have another baby."

"A baby!" Susan gaped at him. "Are you nuts? We've almost got these two raised and you want to start all over again? Oh, no, Hank! If you want to start rebuilding the nest, you're going to have to find another hen to lay the eggs. This one's retired."

"But lots of couples start second families."

"Not us." Susan sat down on the ottoman before her knees gave out on her. Just thinking about having another baby seemed to exhaust her. "You know I love Kim and Jake, Hank. I think we've got the two best kids in the world. I'm not about to press my luck with a third try."

Hank looked at the carpet, staring at the corn rows he was plowing with his bare toes. "It was just an idea."

An idea that had never, ever occurred to Susan. Still reeling from the mere suggestion, she reached out and braced her hand on his slumped shoulder. "But would you really want another baby, Hank?"

Would he? Hank looked up and stared straight into his wife's brown eyes. "I would if I thought that's what it would take to get you back."

"Babies shouldn't be used like that," Susan scolded.

"Well, why not? It's worked before."

"It didn't work very well, or we wouldn't be in the middle of a divorce right now," Susan reminded him.

Hank wasn't daunted. "That can be fixed easily enough. Just say the right words."

Susan shook her head helplessly. "Hank, Hank. What am I going to do with you?"

"Take me back, I hope."

She actually smiled then, sort of. It was a lopsided quirk that made one corner of her mouth go down as the other one went up. Hank recognized it. It was the sort of expression parents had when their kids are being naughty in a cute sort of way. The kind of expression that could slide either way, depending on the kids' next move.

Hank decided to go for broke. "I'm serious, Susan. I want us to start over again."

Susan sighed. "That's what I want, too, Hank. A new beginning. That's why I liked Lara's suggestion so much."

Hank swore beneath his breath. Lara Jamison was one of Susan's oldest friends, and none of her friends liked him. Anything that was her idea couldn't be good news for him. "So what, exactly, is Lara's bright idea?"

"She suggested that you and I begin seeing each other again."

"Seeing each other?"

"You know. Dating."

Hank's mouth opened and closed three times before he was finally able to spit out some words. He swiftly made up for the delay, however. "Dating! That's the stupidest damned idea I've ever heard! We're married, Susan. Married people don't date."

"At least not each other," she agreed. Her meaningful glance wasn't lost on her husband. Hank decided not to take this particular bait. "Fortunately," she continued after a significant pause, "the same rule doesn't apply to people who are legally separated."

"But what's the point?" Hank asked. "Dating each other can't accomplish a damned thing that living together wouldn't solve a whole lot faster."

"Is that what you're going to tell Kim and Jake when they come of age? Don't bother dating, just move on in. If you decide you don't like the person, you can always move out again."

"Of course not!"

"Then why set a bad example for them now?"

"But this isn't the same thing," Hank protested. "Separated or not, Susan, we are still married and by damn, it's high time we started acting like it!"

Susan folded her arms over her chest again, standing tall and resolute. "Sorry, Hank, but that's the best offer you're going to get. Take it or leave it."

11

"WHAT'S HAPPENED to Daddy?"

Hank's daughter stood steadfast in the doorway of her mother's bedroom, clearly prepared to stay until she got a satisfactory answer.

"Is something wrong with him? Is he sick?"

"No, honey. He's fine," her mother mumbled in an intentionally distracted manner, her eyes staying focused on the article she had been editing in bed. When the girl remained fixed in position, Susan reluctantly removed the pencil she had been holding between her teeth and spoke more clearly. "He's fine. Didn't he sound all right when you talked to him on the phone tonight?"

Kim shrugged. "He sounded okay, I guess. But that's not what I mean. Why hasn't he been coming over? He wasn't in church last Sunday and he didn't come to dinner, either. Why not? What happened? Is it something Jake and I did?"

"Of course not. You talk to him on the phone every day, don't you?"

"Well, yeah, but—"

"And he went to every one of your games last week, didn't he?"

"Yes, but it's not the same. I mean, it was almost like he was living here again for a while. What happened?"

"Nothing."

"Mother."

Susan sighed. Why did stubbornness have to be hereditary? "He hasn't been over because I told him to stay away."

"You what?" Kim gaped at her mother. "Why?"

Susan shrugged, trying to make it seem a casual decision. "I needed some space." Did kids nowadays know what that meant?

"Space for what?"

Evidently not. "Space to think."

"I didn't know thinking took up so much room."

"In your father's case it doesn't."

"Mother."

"Sorry—" Susan laughed in spite of herself "—I couldn't resist."

Kim grinned back. "Okay, you're forgiven. But what did you mean? What do you need room to think about?"

"Just things."

Her daughter wasn't satisfied with the vague answer. "What sort of things? Come on, Mom. I have a right to know why you're keeping my own father away from me."

"I'm not trying to keep him away from you. I'm trying to keep him away from me." Susan shook her head as if she were trying to discourage a pesky bug from buzzing in her ear. "Your father's driving me so crazy I can't even think straight anymore."

"Think straight about what?"

"About—" Susan almost fell into the shallow digging. "Never mind. Don't worry about it." She didn't dare get her daughter's hopes up. Kim already seemed to think it was just a matter of time before her father came back to stay. Even Jake seemed to have warmed to the idea. Susan apparently was the only Metcalf still having doubts. Of course, she had enough for all of them.

"You're thinking about getting back together, aren't you?"

So much for not getting hopes up. "I don't know, Kimmie, but it's nothing for you to worry about, okay?" Susan gnawed nervously on the pencil again, desperately wishing her daughter would drop the discussion.

"Don't worry? How can I not worry about the divorce?" Kim shoved aside the pages of news copy, clearing a space for herself on the edge of the bed. "You and Dad aren't the only ones being affected, you know. It matters to me and Jake, too."

"I know, honey. But the final decision has to be made by your father and me."

"Daddy has already decided. He wants to come home. All you have to do is tell him it's okay."

"It isn't that simple."

"Isn't it?" Kim picked up one of her mother's well-chewed pencils and drummed it against the edge of the nightstand. "Daddy is sorry for whatever happened. I'm sure he'll promise to never do anything like it again."

"You don't really believe it's that easy, do you, Kim? He just has to say 'I'm sorry, I won't be bad anymore,' and that's supposed to make everything okay?"

"It could."

"Sorry, pumpkin." Susan brushed her hand across the girl's forehead and tucked a stray wisp of silky dark hair behind Kim's ear. "I guess I'm not that forgiving."

"Yes, you are. Haven't you always told Jake and me that there's nothing we could do that you couldn't forgive? Didn't you mean it when you said that no matter what we did or what kind of trouble we got into, you'd still love us?"

"Yes, of course."

"Then prove it by forgiving Daddy."

"It's not the same thing, Kim." Susan curved her palm against her daughter's high, classic cheekbones. "You and Jake are my children. Whatever mistakes you make, nothing can change that fact. I'll always be here for you."

"But you and Daddy promised to stay married always. Doesn't that mean anything?"

Susan dropped her hands to her lap and stared at her twisting fingers. "I thought it did, but your father broke part of that promise."

"But if he said he was sorry, if he promised not to ever do it again—"

"Promises like that aren't easy to keep, Kimmie. There's no guarantee that he could keep it."

"Can't you give him the chance?" Kim caught her mother's restless hand between her own. "You always give Jake and me a second chance when we mess up. Can't you do the same for Dad?"

Could she?

"You do still love him, don't you?"

Did she? Susan closed her eyes. The air in her lungs escaped in a heartfelt sigh. "I'm thinking about it, okay?"

"You promise?"

"I promise. Now, go get some sleep. It's way past your bedtime."

"That's okay. It's Friday."

Susan felt her daughter tense and knew that she hadn't survived the interrogation yet. "Spill it, Kim. What else is it you want to know?"

"Why have all those men been calling?"

"It's just Aunt Lara's idea of a joke, dear. Ignore them." Susan knew the sudden rise in temperature she felt had nothing to do with the Arkansas delta's volatile spring weather. Damn Lara Jamison's warped sense of humor! She'd get even with her old friend for this one.

"Are you going to go out with any of them?"

"I wouldn't be caught dead with any of them, okay? Stop worrying about it."

Kim still looked doubtful. "Aren't you tempted just a little, though?"

Susan looked at her in surprise. "You wouldn't mind if I dated someone besides your father?"

"Well, sure I'd mind. So would Dad. But I can understand why you might want to. I mean, I can't imagine marrying the first guy I date."

"Good."

"Mother." Kim rolled her eyes. "Come on, I'm being serious. I mean, didn't you ever wonder what it would have been like to be with someone else?"

"Excuse me?"

"It's okay, you can tell me. We've talked about this stuff already, remember? The whole don't-rush-it, wait-till-you're-sure, play-it-safe bit."

Susan arched her eyebrows as only a mother can. "That doesn't sound like you took our talk very seriously. Maybe we should have it again."

"Not necessary. Honest, Mom. I did listen and I do take it seriously. Did you know that two girls in the eighth grade have already had babies? Can you imagine that? Being a mother at my age?" Kim shook her head. "Believe me, I took everything you and Dad told me very seriously."

Susan relaxed a little. "Well, I'm glad to hear that. I know I can't expect you guys to learn everything from our mistakes, but I'd like you to learn at least that much."

"We have," Kim assured her. "That doesn't answer my question, though. Do you wish there'd been other guys besides Daddy?"

Her mother hesitated. It was a question she'd hardly dared to ask herself. "I used to," she admitted finally. "When you're rocking a sick baby while the rest of your class is at the prom, it's a little hard not to wish you had done things differently. I never regretted having you and Jake, though. You two know that, don't you?"

"Sure, Mom. We know. Still, there must have been other times when you wished there had been someone else besides Daddy. I mean, without anything to compare him to, how did you know he was the right one?"

Susan smiled. "Love's not a taste test, honey. You don't have to sample every possibility to decide which one you love best."

Kim pulled her feet up on the bed and crossed her legs, Indian-style. "How can you tell, then? I mean, you and Daddy have hardly anything in common. What made you pick him in the first place?"

"He picked me, actually. You'll have to ask him why. One day he came over and put his football jacket around my shoulders. The next thing I knew we were going steady and then we were married, with a baby on the way."

"But when did you fall in love with him? When did you realize he was the one?"

Susan looked into eyes as black as the ones that had promised to love her always. "I'm not sure there was one particular instant, Kim. It happened over a thousand moments. Just a little bit at a time until one day I found myself saying 'I love you' without being able to remember how many times I had told him before. Sorry, I know that's not very helpful."

"No, not much," Kim agreed.

"It's probably silly of me to try and give you advice anyway," Susan said. "Your father didn't exactly have to beat the competition off with a stick. It was more or less a field of one. You, on the other hand, already have a whole army of admirers."

"Mother."

"It's true and you know it. You're just lucky you took after your father. Although, who'd ever have thought Hank Metcalf would look so good as a girl?"

"Mother!" Both the Metcalf females laughed at the thought of Henry Jacob, Sr. in drag. "Really, Mom," Kim chided again when she had her giggles back under control. "You shouldn't say things like that. Do you know that I always wished I looked like you?"

"Why?" Susan exclaimed, horrified.

"Oh, come on, Mom. You're pretty."

"You're getting your eyes checked tomorrow."

"I mean it," Kim insisted. "I love your hair. I wish mine was curly like yours. And your eyes are so much prettier than mine. Okay, so the left one's always a little off center. It just makes you that much more interesting to look at."

"Right." Her mother looked anything but convinced.

"I mean it. And besides, you got so much style."

Susan laughed. "That's just because the sixties look is coming in again. Believe me, if you had been clothes-conscious two or three years ago, you would have been ashamed to be seen with me."

"No way. I've always loved the way you put things together. You never look like anyone else."

"You know, pumpkin, not everyone would consider that a compliment."

"No. But you do."

Susan was surprised by her daughter's insight. "You're starting to get to know me pretty well, aren't you?"

"I think so," Kim said. "At least, I understand you better than I did a year ago. Working on all these environmental projects has helped. I never understood how the newspaper could mean so much to you until I started working on something that was really important to me."

Susan smiled at the girl. "I feel like I'm really getting to know you, too. And I like what I'm finding out."

"Really?"

"Really. Now, go to bed."

"Okay, okay. I'm gone." Kim hopped off the bed, but bent down to give her mother a quick, hard hug.

"I just want you to know that whatever happens with you and Daddy, I'll still love you, Mom. Even if you make the wrong decision."

"I'LL STILL LOVE YOU, Mom. Even if you make the wrong decision." Kim's voice echoed in the silence long after Susan had switched her own light out. Which would be the wrong decision: taking Hank back or letting him go? "Lord, what should I do?" Susan prayed again and again and again.

She had thought the whole thing was settled when Hank had stormed out of the house on Valentine's Day. Walking out on her once had been bad enough. Walking out twice . . . Well, that was that, as far as she was concerned.

But not as far as Hank was concerned, evidently. He had tried to call her the very next day. She had hung up, of course. She had hung up the day after that, too. Still, he kept calling. Finally, she just started handing the phone over to one of the kids, figuring sooner or later he'd get the message.

Hank showed no signs of letting up. If anything, he seemed to have strengthened his forces. Susan had gone to see Lara Jamison again only to discover that one of her oldest, dearest friends was a damned turncoat.

The lawyer somehow managed to persuade Susan not to push the divorce on through and now the wily blonde had started giving Susan's phone number to the absolute dregs of society. Lara actually had the nerve to say that she thought they were the sort of men that Susan would be attracted to.

"Well, why aren't they?" the attorney had asked when Susan complained. "You said you'd like to find Hank's opposite. This is it, friend. Take it or leave it."

"I was thinking of someone more like Tanner Mc-Neil."

"Back up, girlfriend. He's taken."

"I said 'like him,' didn't I?"

"Sorry," Lara apologized blithely. "He's definitely one of a kind, but I'll keep trying."

"Do me a favor," Susan begged her, "and stop doing me favors."

"But I thought you liked my idea. Don't you want to see what you were missing all these years when you were happily married and your friends were living the swinging single life?"

"I think I'll just reread *Looking for Mr. Goodbar* instead."

"Oh, come on, Susan. You haven't even been on an actual date yet. You can't give up until you've given it a try. How about Walter Simmons? Morticians make good money, you know. I've got his number right here. I can have you fixed up in a jiffy."

"No!" Susan took a deep breath and forced herself to calm down. "Really, Lara, how am I supposed to make time for a date when I couldn't even make time for a husband?"

"Good question. What's the answer?"

The editor-in-chief and publisher of the tricounty biweekly had been completely stumped. "I don't know," she'd confessed weakly. "I'll give you a call when I figure it out."

"Don't waste your dime on me. Call Hank, instead. I think he's the one that needs to know."

It was the only time Susan could ever remember getting mad at the calm, cool, collected woman she'd grown up with. "Whose side are you on, Lara Jamison?"

"JUST WHOSE SIDE are you on, Lara Jamison?" Hank Metcalf asked the attorney. When he had accepted Tanner's invitation to his farm, Metcalf hadn't bargained on McNeil's fiancé showing up. He certainly hadn't expected her to collaborate with them.

"I'm on the side of the Metcalf family. Any complaints?"

Hank slid his gaze warily over to look at Tanner. "Do you really think we can trust her?"

"She wouldn't be here if I didn't."

"Excuse me?" Lara said politely.

Tanner cleared his throat. "I mean, I wouldn't be marrying her if she didn't have my complete trust."

"That's a little better. Now, Hank, here's the plan—"

"You've already got one?" Metcalf interrupted. "I thought we were here to think one up."

"Well, I have a little privileged information, which of course I cannot reveal, but if you'll just trust me . . ."

Hank's gaze slid back over to Tanner, who nodded confidently. "All right. I'm game." Two hours and a severe case of writer's cramp later, Metcalf was beginning to regret his agreement. "Are you two really sure this will work?"

"Positive," Lara said.

Tanner nodded. "All the world loves a lover, right?"

Hank still felt skeptical. "But she's going to know I had help."

"No, she won't."

"How could she?"

Hank frowned at the flowery prose he had scribbled under Tanner and Lara's dictation. "These don't sound at all like the way I talk. You both know that."

"So? Lots of people sound different on paper than they do out loud," Lara pointed out. "Susan will just think there's a side to you she hasn't seen before, which is exactly what we want."

Hank glanced at a couple of the more explicit paragraphs. "I don't know. I think most people who show this side of themselves usually wind up in jail."

Tanner and Lara grinned at each other. "Only if they do them in public," the lawyer told him. "Otherwise it's all perfectly legal."

Metcalf still wasn't convinced. "What if one of the kids reads it by mistake?"

"There's no harm in children realizing their parents are human, too."

Hank reread the first note one more time. The language was beautiful, no doubt about it. And it was certainly effective, judging by the way Tanner and Lara had been eyeing each other. Still, it just didn't sound like him.

"You've changed, Hank. You don't even make love the same anymore."

That clinched it. Hank crumpled the letters in his fist. "No. Sorry, y'all, but it wouldn't work. Susan's already convinced that we're not the same people we were when we fell in love the first time. That's why she's decided there's no hope for us getting back together. Getting a letter like this would only prove that she was right."

"Umm, you may have a point there," Lara admitted. "Susan did say something about your seeming like a stranger. Maybe it would be better if you tried to re-emphasize what it was that brought you together in the first place."

Hank sighed. "I wish I knew what that was. I felt so damned lucky at the time, I never stopped to ask why Susan agreed to go out with me."

"Well, Kim is living proof that you did something right," Tanner pointed out. "We just have to figure out what it was."

"Think back," Lara encouraged. "What did you do before you started shacking up in the back seat?"

Hank shrugged. "Just the usual kid stuff. Games, dances, the drive-in."

"There must have been something else," Tanner prompted. "Something special or someplace only the two of you knew about."

"No." Hank shook his head. The only place he could think of was their usual make-out spot on Rabbit Road, but that wasn't special or secret. The gravel strip that topped one of the levees overlooking the Mississippi River owed its name to the outrageously high conception rate it had achieved over the past fifty years. "I can't think of anything from the past that might help."

"Well, maybe I can do a little subtle digging and unearth a clue from Susan," Lara offered.

Hank looked up hopefully. "Would you?"

"Sure."

He narrowed his gaze and studied the lawyer carefully. "Why the change of heart, Lara? According to Suz, that whole dating bit was your idea. If you weren't sure we belonged together before, what makes you so sure now?"

"I guess I'm just wising up in my old age," Lara said. "It's true," she insisted when Hank and Tanner looked at each other skeptically. "Like most of Susan's friends back in high school, I thought the two of you were too different from each other to make it. I guess I've learned since then that some differences can actually work for the better."

"How so?" Hank asked.

"Well, take you and Susan. The fact that you weren't interested in college was definitely a plus for her. Under the circumstances, it would have been impossible for you both to have gone. If Susan had married anyone else, the odds are that she would have been the one to put him through school. Because you were willing to support her, she was able to get her degree and become a damn good journalist. And, unlike a lot of career women, Susan didn't have to choose between family and job."

"I don't know," Hank said after a moment. "I think Susan has too much ink in her blood to have let anything stop her from becoming a reporter. As for having a family, well, that wasn't exactly a conscious decision."

"Kim may not have been preplanned," Laura conceded, "but she was free choice. Susan had other options to choose from, Hank. She went against all advice when she picked marriage to you. I think that says something."

"Maybe it did back then." Hank stood slowly and put on his cap. "I don't think it has much bearing on the present, though. Not as far as Susan is concerned."

"I'm not too sure about that," said Lara. "Some things may have changed, but the basics are still there. You and Susan managed to hang in there for a long time, Hank. You must have been doing something right. Your best bet may be to figure out what that something was and put it back into practice."

Hank tugged the bill of his cap down to shade his eyes. "I'll try. If you find out anything . . ."

"I'll call," she promised. "But it's up to you in the end. And by the way, I still think dating each other would be a good idea. If nothing else, it would at least force Susan to start scheduling some private time for the two of you. I'd think you'd be all for that."

Actually, the idea of having to schedule time with his wife had been one of the things Hank had disliked about their marriage. But as he lay in his bed that night staring at the ceiling of his motel room, Hank thought back over his early days with Susan and began to reconsider that particular peeve.

Plotting ways around curfews and parental interference had been part of the excitement they had felt in high school. After a good deal of trial and error, they had finally perfected their means of escape. On the given night at the specified hour, Hank would sneak around the back of the Mitchum house with a handful of pea gravel....

12

SUSAN THOUGHT she was imagining at first. Then the sound came again, a tapping on her window. But that was impossible—she was on the second floor. It couldn't be a branch; there were no trees directly outside her room. The sound was too sharp to be rain.

Tap, tap, tap. There it went again.

Freeing herself from the tangled bedclothes, she tiptoed across to the window seat and gently parted the curtains. There was only a sliver of moon, but the stars were shining brightly. Susan leaned forward so that her forehead almost touched the glass, and peered down into the backyard.

Tap, tap, tap. Instinctively she jumped back as something struck the pane again. Something small. Small enough not to nick the glass. It couldn't be, she thought. She yanked up the window and leaned over the sill.

"Hank? Is that you?"

One shadow separated from the others. "Shh," it whispered. "Don't wake the children."

"What the hell do you think you're doing?"

"Shh!" The shadow shushed her again before disappearing into the night.

What the heck was that man up to? Susan hurriedly pulled on a pair of jeans to go with the oversize T-shirt she was wearing and jammed her feet into a pair of sneakers. *Sneaking around at*—she glanced at the digital clock on her dresser—*two o'clock in the morning!* "That's it," she told herself. "I'm calling the state mental-health department tomorrow. He has to be certifiable."

She marched out into the backyard, her hands perched on her hips. "Do you know what time it is?" she asked when he emerged once more from the shadows. "Let me tell you. It's two o'clock in the damned morning! What on earth are you doing out here throwing pebbles at two o'clock in the damned morning?"

"Shh." Hank placed a finger to his lips, then took a side step, bowing to his right, one arm sweeping out in a grand gesture to indicate the quilt he had spread out on the ground. "Just step this way and you'll find out."

It was the very same quilt, Susan realized. Or at least an identical one. Suddenly the reasons for Hank's visit became crystal clear. "I told you, no more trips down memory lane. That's not the answer, Hank."

"Maybe not," he admitted, "but it's a place to start. You said you wanted us to date, to get to know each other. Well, this is the best way I can think of. Come on, Susan. Lie down with me."

She held her stance, swaying slightly as she felt the blood rushing through her veins. "A little moonlight necking wasn't what I had in mind."

"It's not what I have in mind, either." *Not entirely, anyway.* The pale light glinted off Hank's strong, white teeth. "I still have a few surprises left, Suz. This one you'll enjoy. Trust me."

She hesitantly accepted the hand he held out. "This had better be good, Henry Jacob."

"It will be the best." He led her over to the quilt, then gently tugged her down beside him. Stretching out on his back, Hank gestured for her to do the same. "Just lie down and relax. You can even close your eyes if you want. I'll tell you when to open them."

She did as she was told, wondering idly which star he would choose tonight. It had been so long since he had taken her stargazing, since he had spread the quilt out for the first time and asked her to lie down beside him.

Susan couldn't remember the stars' names anymore, but she wasn't surprised that Hank did. Sky watching had been his expertise, not hers. And, truth be told, she had been much more interested in the other lessons they had taught each other as they had lain beneath a black velvet blanket, studded with diamond lights.

"Now!" Hank exclaimed suddenly. "Open your eyes, Snookums. Look!"

A flickering light caught her attention and Susan looked up just in time to spot a burst of red sparks, one followed quickly by another and then another as silent fireworks rained across the sky. "Oh, Hank!"

"You like?"

"You know I do." Susan squeezed her fingers around his and gasped with pleasure as another meteor burst through space, millions of miles away.

Hank rolled over on his side, facing her. "Still mad at me?"

"For waking me up?" Susan shook her head, keeping her focus on the heavens above for more showers of light. "No, I'm not mad."

"What about—"

"What are y'all doing out here?"

The couple jerked up as one. "Jake! Kim!"

Their children took another step forward. "What's going on out here?" Jake demanded again. "Are you okay, Mom?"

Susan hadn't felt this guilty or embarrassed since her father had snuck up on them armed with a flashlight and a shotgun. "I'm fine, son. We're just watching the stars, that's all."

Jake didn't look any more convinced than Mr. Mitchum had. "Are you sure you're okay, Mom?"

"She's fine," Hank answered for his wife. "There's a meteor shower tonight. I just thought your mother might like to watch it."

"A meteor shower! Really?" Jake forgot his duties as self-appointed guardian.

"Yes, really. Come here and watch for yourself," Susan invited. "You, too, Kim. Come on. We'll make room." She started to scoot over to the far side of the blanket, but was checked by Hank's firm grip on her hand, and found herself being maneuvered against his side instead. The children stretched out on either side of them, squeezing her even closer to their father.

It wasn't what he had planned, but Hank chose to make the best of the situation. He put an arm around Susan's shoulders, providing a resting place for her head, and held her firm.

His wife wriggled uncomfortably. They were much too close. Instead of loosening his hold, however, Hank held her tighter. When she squirmed again, he strengthened his hold even more. Susan started to speak out, then closed her mouth, forcing herself to lie still as the tension in her husband's rigid body finally communicated his own dire predicament.

As Jake and Kim oohed and aahed over the fire bursts in the sky, Susan choked on a fit of giggles. The first time she and Hank had lain on this quilt to watch the stars, the fireworks in heaven had led to heaven on earth. She had no doubt that Hank had been hoping for a reenactment. Fortunately for her, he had forgotten to take into account that children make much better chaperons than parents.

THE GLOW-IN-THE-DARK watch face caught Hank's eye as he traced yet another star pattern in the air with his finger. The minute hand had almost passed the hour at the three o'clock position. "That's it for tonight, kids. It's been half an hour since the last meteor shower. Show's over."

"Not yet, Dad," Jake groaned. "It'd be like leaving in the middle of a movie. Can't we just sleep out here for the rest of the night? You can show us some more constellations if the showers don't start again."

Hank grasped the boy's hand, hauling the lad to his feet. "To bed, Jake. You can still get four hours or so of sleep. Now, go on."

"But tomorrow's Sunday. I don't have school."

"Today is Sunday, and you do have church." As Kim and Susan stood also, Hank picked up the quilt. "Besides, we're really not equipped to spend the whole night out here. Next time we'll have to be better prepared. I need something more than this between me and the cold hard ground."

"It's not that cold," Jake protested.

"Not to your young bones maybe, but it is to mine. I know a place in Memphis that sells used camping gear. We'll have to take a trip over there and get some sleeping bags, maybe even a small tent. Then we could go to Village Creek State Park and camp out all night."

"Really? All night?" Jake's eyes brightened eagerly.

"When?" Kim wanted to know. "Tomorrow?"

"The store wouldn't even be open tomorrow," Hank reminded them. "I'm afraid it'll have to wait till next Saturday."

"Aww, Dad."

"Hey, you two." Susan laughed. "It's just one week. It won't kill you to wait that long." But neither child perked up much. "Look at it this way. Now you'll have a whole week to bone up. We'll go to the library on Monday and check some books out for you."

"You think our library will have many books on space and stuff?" Jake asked skeptically.

"I'd bet on it," Hank said, making a mental note to get there first and do a little studying of his own.

"And what you don't find there, I bet you could find at the Planetarium at the Pink Palace Museum in Memphis." Susan cast a speculative glance at her husband. "I bet your dad might be persuaded to include that as a stop on your trip to Memphis."

"Would you, Dad?" Kim and Jake asked together.

"Sounds good to me." Hank looked questioningly at his wife. "But are you sure you can spare the time from the newspaper, Susan."

"Me?"

"Can you, Mom?" Jake begged.

"Please," Kim added.

Susan looked from one face to another. Each anxious, each hopeful, each depending on her. "I'll make time."

"Then it's a date," Hank confirmed with relief.

A date? His wife smiled. "Yes, I guess it is."

Pacified at last, Jake and Kim allowed themselves to be sent to bed. As they disappeared into the house, Hank placed a strong arm across Susan's shoulders and gave his wife a warm, firm squeeze. "Thanks," he whispered huskily, ignoring the way she tensed at the contact.

"What for? It was your idea."

"Yeah, but you could have shot it down. You didn't."

Susan shrugged and stepped away from him. "Why should I have? I haven't seen Kim and Jake this excited about anything in a long time. Kim will probably lose all interest in the recycling project now."

"There's no reason they can't do both." Hank took a step, too, staying close. "We can make them family projects, just as we talked about in the negotiations. It's about time we started doing things together."

"'It's past time' might be more accurate." Susan tried once more to increase the distance between them.

"Not necessarily." Again Hank moved with her, pressing against her back. "Remember how we always used to say we'd take a family vacation and make up for lost time, but the vacation plans always fell through?"

Susan nodded cautiously. "I remember."

"We should have just forgotten about the big trips and concentrated on enjoying the things that were right here. Like the Planetarium. I've been wanting to go there for years. Every time I go into Memphis I think, 'Save it for the next trip,' and so I've never gone."

"Same here." Susan turned halfway toward him, regret shimmering in her eyes. "There were all kinds of things I wanted us to do with the kids, but I was always too busy. I kept thinking, 'next year.' Now they're too old to enjoy a lot of them.

"I guess that's what I did with you, too," she confessed. "I knew we weren't spending enough time together, but I kept telling myself I would make up for it later. I took it for granted that you'd still be here."

Hank grasped her shoulders, drawing her into his embrace. "I am still here."

"No. Not really."

"I could be. I want to be." One arm slid down and around her waist as he raised his other hand to trace the soft curve of her jaw. "We'll take it as slow as you like, Susan. If you want us to date, that's what we'll do. Whatever it takes, honey, I'll do it."

He could feel her chin quivering, feel her clench her teeth to make it stop. "Please, Susan. Give us another chance." He lowered his head until their lips were almost touching, then stopped, waiting for her to meet him.

Susan arched her neck. Her mouth grazed his, but she jerked her head back the instant he started to deepen the kiss.

"Slow and easy, Hank. Slow and easy."

PROCEED WITH CAUTION became Susan's motto. Her mother would have been proud of her—if Susan had followed the same creed when she was a teen. In some ways, Susan wished she had.

She and Hank had been in too much of a hurry to solve all the mysteries when they were young to enjoy the sort of delicious anticipation building between them now. At least, Susan was enjoying it. She'd seen more movies in the past month than she had in the past ten years. Not to mention the dinners out and field trips to the Memphis museums and zoo.

Although she had been safely chaperoned by her children on most occasions, Hank always managed to get her alone for at least a few minutes of heavy petting. And now and then, he even managed to steal her away for a whole evening.

Last night, Hank must have decided to give nostalgia another try. He'd driven her down Rabbit Road, dodging several cars of teenage lovebirds to nab their favorite parking spot on the levee.

Only the view had changed since they had come as teens themselves. Two bridges now crossed the river dividing Arkansas and Tennessee. The new bridge formed a giant stylized *M*, boldly lit up to introduce the river city. The Memphis skyline had grown taller, broader and more sophisticated with the addition of the new Pyramid, its shimmering silhouette of light reflecting in the dark water of the Mississippi.

"Has it changed that much?" Susan whispered to Hank. "Or did I just forget how beautiful the view was?"

"I couldn't tell you," her husband answered honestly. "I don't remember looking at the view when we were here before. We were pretty busy with other things, remember?"

"Umm. It makes you wonder what else we didn't see." Susan sighed. "Perhaps that's one of the advantages of aging. Now, we can slow down and take time to appreciate things without all the rush-rush, hurry-up, let's-do-it business."

"Maybe." Hank unbuckled his shoulder harness and leaned toward her, sliding one arm around her shoulders. "Personally speaking, though, I think the rush-rush had a few merits I wouldn't mind exploring again."

Susan smiled, relaxing comfortably against him without the slightest trace of jitters. "Oh, it wouldn't be the same now. I mean, what's a little rush-rush after you've had the luxury of a real bed and sleeping together all night. I wouldn't want you to be let down, Hank."

"Trust me," he said, pressing closer. "I could use a little letting down right now."

She slid one hand up his thigh to measure his truth, ignoring the sudden gnashing of his teeth. "Umm, you may have a point there. Maybe if I just lower this a bit you'd be more comfortable."

Hank clamped her wrist with one hand, forcing her fingers to halt their assault on the zipper of his blue jeans. "Don't," he begged her, suddenly regretting the impulse that had brought them to the levee. "Susan, don't start something you're not going to finish. I can't take it tonight."

"Sure you can, tough guy." The zipper slipped down five notches.

"I'm serious, Suz." His voice was growing deeper, thicker with need. "You're going to tease me to my death if you're not careful."

"Nonsense," she assured him as the zipper gave way completely. "That's just a myth."

"And you're a sadist," Hank declared as she made short work of his belt buckle and the button securing his waistband. "You're just enjoying this because I'm suffering so much. How could I have been married to you this long and not realized I was married to a sadist?"

Her fingers slipped inside the opening she had created, leading him free from the confines of clothing. "Do you want me to stop now?"

"No," he groaned, as she imprisoned him again, this time in the warm cocoon of her hand. "I want to go all the way. Full speed ahead. Fire the torpedoes."

Susan studied him carefully as the cocoon began to pulse around him, squeezing and stroking in a rhythm that quickened, then slowed in alternate measures.

Hank's eyes closed. His jaw locked shut, grinding his teeth together. Shudders racked his body. He was too rigid with need to absorb the unbearable pleasure with which she tortured him.

Each reaction fed Susan's growing sense of power and her daring. She was going to drive him to the limits and over the edge. Her lips pressed against his throat, then skidded down to his chest as her free hand made short work of his shirt buttons. She kissed her way down his body until her lips were beside the hand that held him, ready to shift into high gear.

"For God's sake," Hank pleaded harshly when she hesitated. "Don't stop now. If you have any mercy at all, Susan, don't stop now."

Her fingers unfolded, abandoning the stretch of satiny skin over taut muscle to the warm dampness of her mouth. Hank jerked in his seat. He grasped the steering wheel, desperate for something to hold on to, bracing himself for the head-on collision.

When the full impact hit, it sent him flying, tumbling, spinning what seemed a hundred yards. When he finally reopened his eyes, Hank was amazed to find himself still in the front seat, his wife smiling at him. "Am I still alive?"

"Definitely."

"Good. I was afraid I wasn't going to get the chance to reciprocate." He made a lethargic lunge, which Susan easily dodged.

"That's okay," she assured him. "I'll take a rain check. It's time to go home."

"We've still got a little time left."

Susan shook her head. "You know how strict Jake is about that curfew."

"Just wait till it's his turn," Hank vowed. "I'm taking notes."

He walked her to the front door just as the clock began to chime the midnight hour. He held her in the glow of the porch light, tilting her face up for one last kiss. Their lips touched softly, lingering, parting slowly.

"So when do I get a chance to pay you back?" Hank whispered.

"Let's just call it a freebie."

"But I want to show my appreciation."

"I think you showed it pretty well tonight."

"Susan..."

"Besides," she soothed him, "I already have our next date planned."

"Oh, really?"

"Yep. Just meet me at the office tomorrow afternoon, about one o'clock."

"Your office? What are we going to do there?"

"Meet me tomorrow and find out."

"THIS IS YOUR IDEA of a date?" Hank asked as he looked around the *Gazette*'s office the next afternoon. They were all alone. The typewriters sat quietly beneath their dustcovers. The floor felt solid and still. The vibrations of the presses had been quieted with the flick of a switch after the last Saturday Shopper's edition had been run off.

"Let me guess," he leered with a hopeful expression. "The printing press is really just a cover for the torture chamber you've been hiding in the basement and you've been waiting for the right moment to lure me down there and have your wicked way."

Susan laughed. "Who ever said I was the one with the imagination? Look, I thought that if I gave you the grand tour and showed you how things ran here, you wouldn't feel so left out when I have to work."

She stood on tiptoe and plopped a fleeting kiss on his mouth. "I don't want the *Gazette* to come between us, Hank. I don't want to have to choose between marriage and career."

"I haven't asked you to," Hank protested.

"No?" Susan asked. "What was that little temper tantrum you threw the other day when I had to cancel out on dinner."

"I don't throw temper tantrums."

"Of course you don't, dear." Susan stroked the lower lip he was sticking out with a gentle finger. "The point is, you were very upset. I could feel it. I had nightmares about it. I could just see us repeating the past nine months over and over. I can't live with that, Hank. If we get back together you're going to have to accept my career."

"I do accept it." Hank grasped her hands and held them tightly in his own. "Sure, I don't like being stood up, but I understand . . . usually."

Susan arched her eyebrows as he tacked on the last word. She knew things had been going too smoothly.

"Hell, Suz," Hank hurried on, realizing he'd made a mistake. "I'm damned proud of what you do and how well you do it. What do you think attracted me in the first place?"

"I've always wondered," his wife admitted. "Why did you ask me to that dance?"

"Because I—" Hank hesitated, fumbling for the right words. Before he could find them, the front door opened to admit two gangly teens, one male, one female.

They were dressed identically in faded jeans, denim jackets and clean T-shirts. Pencils were jammed behind their ears, pocket-size notebooks peeked out of their breast pockets. Twin straps stretched across their chests, supporting the basic manual 35mm cameras resting like sidearms against their hips.

Susan took a step back to dispel the intimacy of her position next to Hank and began preparing her standard rejection. These two were tenacious. She had to give them that much credit.

"Afternoon, Mrs. Metcalf," the girl began. "Sir," she added tactfully. "I hope we're not disturbing anything."

Susan's smile was gentle. "Of course not, Penny. What can I do for you?"

"George and I were just wondering if you had any openings yet. We're willing to do anything."

"I'm sorry, hon," the publisher answered softly, "I'm afraid I still have a full staff. But keep checking back. You never know."

"You wouldn't have to pay us," the boy inserted quickly. "We'd be willing to start off for free. Sort of an internship, you know."

"That's a very tempting offer, George." Susan was still smiling as she walked over to the door and opened it again for their exit. "I'll call if I decide to take you up on it. Y'all have a nice afternoon, now."

"Yes, ma'am. Thank you." The pair disappeared as quickly and quietly as they had arrived.

As the door closed behind them, Hank stared at his wife. "You turned down free labor? You keep telling me you're overworked because you're understaffed and yet you turn down free labor?"

"You get what you pay for," Susan reminded him. "Those two are just high school sophomores. They haven't even finished Journalism 101. Training them to be useful would be more work."

"How much training do you need to roll newspapers or stuff flyers?"

Susan laughed. "Those two think they're the next Woodward and Bernstein. They won't settle for menial tasks like that."

"They said they'd do anything." Hank walked over to the window and watched the teenagers shuffle down the sidewalk. "Let them prove it. If Penny and George are sharp enough to pick things up, you'd have yourself a couple of dedicated workers."

"Did they hire you as their agent or something?" Susan asked, joining him by the window. "What difference does it make to you?"

"It would make a big difference if they took even a little of the work load off you. Besides, they remind me of a couple of other kids I used to know." He draped an arm across her shoulders. "Where would we be if Joe and Buddy hadn't taken a chance on me?

"And how about the break Sam Symond gave you?" he added, turning her to face him. "You were probably the same age as Penny when you came to him begging for a chance to prove yourself on the *Gazette*. Don't you feel some sort of obligation to pass on the torch?"

"I suppose so," Susan hedged.

"Hell, Suz. Those kids could learn more just by watching you than they could in a hundred journalism classes."

"Thanks for the vote of confidence."

"I mean it," Hank said. "I've always been proud of what you do and how well you do it. That's why I'd never ask you to give up the newspaper or journalism."

He circled his arms loosely around her. "You wanted to know why I asked you out that first time. It was because I admired you. You were so driven, even back then. You always had that pencil behind your ear, just like Penny did, and a little notebook jammed in your pocket. There was a sense of purpose about you, Susan. And everyone knew you had the stuff to make it happen."

Hank shrugged self-consciously. "I guess I was hoping some of it would rub off on me."

"Incredible," Susan said. "There I was, worrying about the loveless fate of girls who wear glasses, and a football player actually asked me out because he respected my brain."

How many times had he thanked heaven for those glasses? Hank wondered. Competition was the last thing he'd ever needed. He tightened his hold, squeezing her gently. "So why did you say yes?"

She leaned her forehead against his chest and confessed somewhat shamefully, "I thought you were cute."

Hank grinned and waited for her to elaborate. When she didn't, his smile slid into an incredulous gape. "That's it? You thought I was cute?"

"Still do," she whispered huskily.

He dropped his arms, clucking at her with disappointment. "Talk about role reversal. See, it's all your fault. All I ever wanted was to be loved for my mind, and women just want my body."

There was a long pause, then Susan lifted her head, challenge in her eyes.

"Women? Just how many are we talking here, Hank?"

"Uh, didn't you say something about a tour?"

"The torture chamber's right this way."

13

"THE KEY INGREDIENT in a good journalist is good instincts—being able to smell the smoke before anyone spots the fire, knowing something is news before the rest of the world is aware it exists."

Susan leaned back against the desk and eyed her newest staff members skeptically. "That's what you two are going to have to show me. Good instincts. Prove you've got them and I'll give you a paycheck and a byline. But you have to show me first. Understand?"

"Yes, ma'am!" Penny practically shouted.

George grinned. "You bet, chief."

Susan smothered a smile. Lois Lane and Jimmy Olsen hadn't had as much enthusiasm as these two. "Well, what are you waiting for, then? Get out there and bring me some stories.

"The high school is your beat," she reminded them as they scrambled out of their chairs. "See what you can dig up on those senior profiles I mentioned to you. And try to get some good candids," she added, glancing at their cameras. "I want something more interesting than those posed senior portraits."

"Will do, chief!"

Susan felt good as she watched them dash out of the room. Better than good. She felt strong, powerful. She laughed a little, then, wondering what George and Penny would think if they knew they were the first employees she had ever hired. The rest of the *Gazette*'s staff had been inherited along with the presses, the typewriters, the building and the base circulation.

Maybe that's what was making her feel so good. It had been her decision. Hank might have given her the nudge, but it had been her decision. And there was no one around to veto it. No one around to second-guess her.

Susan looked around the private office that had been Sam Symond's private domain for thirty-five years. It had taken months for her to stop looking for him over her shoulder. It had taken even longer for her to work up the nerve to write the stories and run the editorials her former boss would have forbidden.

Once, the morning after Sam's retirement party, she had come into the *Gazette* early, before anyone else arrived, crept into this office and pulled out the chair behind Sam's desk. The drawers had already been emptied. Sam's family pictures had been taken down. Only his presence had lingered like the scent of the Cuban cigars he was forever smoking, hanging in the air like a ghost.

Susan had chased off the silly notion. Sam wasn't dead, after all. He was on his way to Florida where he had a dockside condominium and a brand-new fishing boat waiting, all paid for with the hefty bank loan Susan had taken out for the purchase of the *Gazette*.

Reassured by the thought of the bank note that proclaimed her ownership of the newspaper, she had worked up the courage to ease into Sam's chair, leaning back slowly, flicking ashes off an invisible cigar. Then she leaned back farther, tilting up her chin, breathing a long stream of air, visualizing the smoke curling toward the ceiling, and smiling with satisfaction.

"So," Susan had mimicked Sam's gruff voice, "you think we should be more aggressive, do you?"

"Yes, sir," she had responded in her own voice.

"You think we should put more bite in the editorials, take a real stand?"

"Yes, sir. I do."

"Well, who the hell do you think you are, young lady? The publisher?"

Susan had grinned, lifting her hands to her chest, wrapping her fingers around imaginary suspenders, raising her feet up to prop them on the desk. "Yes, sir, I—"

The chair had flipped over with a crash, spilling Susan onto the floor. She had glanced wildly around for wily old Sam and seen nothing but the journalism awards he had left on the walls mocking her insubordination. How dare she think she could be publisher?

She had run out of the office as if demons were on her tail. When the rest of the staff had come in, they had found Susan sitting at her old desk, slaving away as usual.

When someone had asked when she was going to move into Sam's office, she had shrugged and said, "Whenever the stink of those cigars evaporates."

The crew had all laughed and no one had mentioned it since.

Even knowing that Sam was alive and well, fishing off the Florida coast, hadn't kept Susan from seeing his ghost in the office or from feeling his unblinking stare reading over her shoulder, chopping her stories before she'd even finished writing them.

Consequently, Susan had worked twice as hard, editing herself more harshly than Sam ever had. Gradually she'd given herself permission to try something new—a different angle, a more controversial story. Still, it had taken nine months and a ten-percent increase in circulation and advertising revenues before she had worked up the nerve to take Sam's name off the *Gazette*'s masthead.

Even then, she hadn't had the courage to put her name in his place as publisher and editor-in-chief. She had simply let the newspaper hierarchy begin with "Susan Mitchum Metcalf, News Editor"—the position she'd held for the previous ten years.

Susan had only chosen to use Sam's office this morning because she'd felt that an employment interview demanded privacy. Now, still feeling the flush of power from her first hiring, she took a deep breath and realized the air didn't smell like cigars anymore.

Walking slowly around the big oak desk, Susan pulled out the ancient leather chair, easing into it as if she still expected someone to pull it out from under her. Leaning back, her hands grasping the armrests lightly, she stretched out her legs and gently propped her feet on top of the desk.

She took a deep breath and released her grip, leaning back even more, folding her arms behind her head. She closed her eyes, sighed and began to relax.

"Looks like I'm going to have a little competition."

Susan jerked in her seat, pictured herself crashing to the floor again. Her eyes flashed open. The world righted itself. She locked her fingers together behind her head and took a deep breath as she spotted David Sinclair filling the open doorway.

"Just trying to keep you on your toes," Susan told the young man who had been her lone reporter until now. She took another breath, forcing herself to relax back in the chair. Nobody was going to dump her out this time.

"George and Penny may be green as grass, but they are eager," she continued. "I think they'll work out quite well."

"I'm sure they will," David told her. "It'll be nice to have a little new blood to liven up the old place."

"My thoughts exactly." Susan forced a smile, realizing she had sounded a bit defensive. *You're the boss,* she reminded herself. *You don't need anyone's permission.*

As if to prove her point, she made another decision on the spot. "You know, with the staff expanding, I could use a little more help on the editorial end. How would you feel about a promotion, Dave?"

"What?"

"I was thinking maybe news editor. How does that grab you? Of course, there would be a small raise."

Stunned, David stared at her. "Are you serious?"

"Unless you prefer just being a reporter?"

"No, I'll take it. Thanks." He shook off his amazement. "Thank you very much."

"You've earned it," his employer declared. "You can take my old desk. Penny and George can share the table you were using."

"Great." David started to back out the door, as if he wanted to get away before she changed her mind.

"You realize this means Penny and George are your responsibility?" Susan continued before he could disappear. "You'll make their assignments and ensure they follow through. Think you can handle that?"

"Of course," he answered automatically, still retreating. Then he stopped, the full magnitude of his new power sinking in. "I mean, yes, ma'am. I won't let you down."

"I know you won't," Susan said. "Oh, and David, update the masthead for Tuesday's issue."

David grinned. "You bet, chief."

Susan shook her head as he made his exit. Chief. Obviously, David had overheard George's comment.

Terrific, she thought. *Another pet name.* Wasn't the firehouse dog named Chief? Oh, well it was better than Snookums. In fact, she even kind of liked it. After all, she was the editor-in-chief of the *Gazette,* as well as the publisher. And if it was good enough for Superman's boss, it ought to be good enough for her.

Yes, Chief would do just fine. Maybe she could even get Hank to make the switch. It was certainly better than any of the other suggestions he had come up with.

She'd found his obsession with pet names rather unsettling until Hank had explained about the Carlsons. She supposed if June Carlson didn't object to being called an insect, she shouldn't have a problem with being named after a dog.

It was kind of sweet of Hank, really. Wanting them to have special names for each other was romantic. The practice certainly hadn't hurt her own parents' marriage.

I wonder how they came up with their names, Susan mused. Patty-Cake was obviously derived from her mother's name, which was Patricia. *But where did Mom get the idea to call Dad Admiral? He wasn't even in the navy.*

Susan made a mental note to ask her mother the next time they met. Then on second thought, she scribbled a memo for her part-time features writer and stuck it in Carol's box. "Check out unusual nicknames couples have for each other. Is there any tie between having special names and marital happiness? Might lead in to other secrets for keeping romance in a marriage. Good feature possibility for the wedding supplement."

"June brides." Susan sighed. Early summer was the traditional time for weddings, particularly in the delta region where people still tended to marry young, generally in the summer months following high school or college graduation. She had been a July bride, although her marriage license had predated her high school diploma by a year.

Fourteen years. She sighed again. As their anniversary date drew closer, Hank was pressing harder and harder for a full reconciliation. "What better time to make it official?" he had pointed out.

It's been a good day for decisions, Susan reflected. Maybe it was time she made this one. She glanced at her calendar: five weeks until their anniversary. Then a red circle around the fifteenth of June caught her eye. Only two weeks left until Lara's wedding.

Damn, Susan thought. She couldn't be happier for Lara Jamison. Her best friend deserved a second chance at happiness and there wasn't a better man for Lara than Tanner McNeil. She'd been thrilled when Lara had asked her to be the matron of honor. Unfortunately, her friend had failed to inform her that Tanner had asked Hank to be his best man until after Susan had committed herself.

Everyone at the wedding would be watching the Metcalfs for signs of a reconciliation even as they listened to the bride and groom's promises to love and cherish, forsaking all others. *How ironic*, Susan thought without appreciation. *How embarrassing*.

THE MORNING of the wedding, Susan entered the Jamison family's kitchen, still yawning and rubbing the sleep out of her eyes. She, Lara and the bridesmaid, Kelly Ryan, the third member of the exclusive triangle of friendship formed in high school, had held a slumber party at Lara's house the night before for old times' sake.

Calculating how much sleep she had missed, Susan groaned and started a pot of strong coffee. The exhaustion she felt now would be nothing compared to how tired she would be after Lara and Tanner's wedding.

When the coffee had finished brewing, she poured herself a mug and sat down on one of the stools beside the breakfast bar. It was too late to back out now.

"Couldn't sleep either, eh?"

Susan jumped at the unexpected sound of another voice.

"Sorry," Lara apologized in a whisper as she poured herself a cup of coffee. "I didn't mean to startle you."

"That's okay," Susan assured her quickly. "My mind is in such a clutter that I didn't hear you get up. What's the matter? Bridal jitters?"

Lara smiled with a confidence Susan envied. "No. Just excitement. This time I know there isn't anything to be jittery about."

"But isn't it even scarier the second time around?" Susan bit her lip. "I'm sorry. I shouldn't even ask something like that on your wedding day."

"I don't mind." The bride-to-be seemed to take no offense. "I thought it would be scarier myself, but it's not. I guess because I know that this time is different.

"Don't get me wrong," Lara inserted quickly. "It's not that I expect everything between us to be perfect all the

time. I just know that Tanner and I have what it takes
to work our way through whatever happens."

"And you and your first husband didn't?"

"No," Lara answered honestly. "We didn't. My marriage to Kevin was almost a matter of convenience. We
were good company when we had time to spend together, and when we didn't, neither of us really minded.
Actually, we were really more like roommates than
husband and wife. There was no sharing, no real commitment involved."

"But there is with Tanner?"

"Absolutely." Lara's face lit up at the mention of her
future husband. "We'll both demand a lot, but we'll also
give two hundred percent. I think that's what it takes
to make a good marriage."

"But what if something were to happen?" Susan
probed cautiously. "Do you really believe there isn't the
slightest chance you would ever divorce him?"

Lara smiled. "I know it's hard to believe, coming
from a divorce attorney—particularly when I'm your
divorce attorney—but yes, I really do believe there is
nothing we can't work out."

"But what if . . ."

"What if I thought Tanner had betrayed me?"

Susan nodded once. "Yes, what if that happened?"

"Then I have Tanner's own permission to beat him
over the head with a cast-iron skillet until the sweet
light of reason is once more shining in that bright mind
of his."

"Is that what you advise me to do?"

Lara shook her head. "In your case, I don't think the
frying pan is necessary. I've gotten to know Hank much
better since Tanner and I started seeing each other.
Whatever led him astray to start with, I believe he is

genuinely repentant now. But it's still your choice, Susan. Nobody can make you forgive him. It has to be your decision."

"Forgiving him isn't the hard part," Susan said slowly. "I guess if you love someone enough you can forgive them anything. It's just that I'm afraid. What if I take him back and then it happens again, only this time he goes through with it?"

Susan bowed her head, wringing her hands together as she finally voiced the fear she hadn't wanted to admit. "I feel as if by forgiving him and taking him back, I'm saying it was okay."

"But you aren't," Lara assured her. "Forgiving doesn't equal condoning."

"Not to us, maybe," Susan said. "But I'm not sure men recognize the difference."

"Then it's up to you to make sure Hank does recognize it," Lara told her. "I don't think it will be a problem, Susan. He has certainly proven over the last two months that he's willing to do anything to get you back."

"I know." Susan ran one finger idly around the edge of her mug. "It's been wonderful. I think we've spent more time together during these past few weeks of dating than we have in the last ten years of a marriage. I'm just afraid it won't continue after he moves back in."

"It can if you're willing to make the time. There's no law that says two people who live together can't date each other. You and Hank have to keep scheduling each other in." Lara hesitated for a moment. "Suz, if you really want my personal advice, as your friend not as your lawyer..."

"Please, tell me. What would you do?"

"Go for it. The sooner, the better."

SEVERAL HOURS LATER, Lara stood beaming radiantly as she prepared to be joined with her new husband. The bride showed no signs of her lack of sleep. Susan, on the other hand, felt as if she were going to fold up like one of the guest chairs that had been arranged in neat rows in Tanner's garden.

Mrs. Jamison and Lara's older sisters were running around like mother hens after the one poor little chick they all had to share. Tanner's older sister had cornered the judge and was giving him instructions regarding the ceremony. The rest of the men had been tempering their own nerves with samplings of champagne. All in all, it was enough to make Susan very glad she and Hank had eloped.

At last, the wedding began. Susan marched down the makeshift aisle behind Kelly, their matching pale blue taffeta dresses appearing like a patch of clear sky against the background of the rose-covered gazebo being used as an altar. Everything was beautiful, planned to perfection.

Susan listened carefully to the ceremony the couple had written themselves and was not ashamed of the mist that suddenly clouded her vision. She knew there wouldn't be a dry eye present after the heartfelt promises were exchanged.

She lifted her head to keep the tears from streaking down her carefully made-up face, bringing her watery gaze into direct eye contact with Hank.

He didn't say a word to disturb the wedding in progress. He didn't have to. He spoke to his wife in the intimate, silent language developed and perfected through their long years of courtship and marriage.

14

WE COULD BE LIKE THEM. Hank's eyes darted from his wife to the happy couple and back again.

Hush! Susan flashed back.

But we love each other as much as they do. He persisted.

Now isn't the time to discuss it. She glared at him.

Won't you give me another chance? His firm mouth drooped woefully at the corners, pleading.

Susan's chin thrust out belligerently. *I haven't decided, yet. We'll talk about it later. Not now.*

He lifted one brow dubiously. *Really? How do I know you aren't just saying that?*

His wife's brows were perfectly level, her mouth slightly pinched. *Because I don't say what I don't mean. Now, hush.*

Hank's face was impassive for a moment. Then he cocked his head a little to one side. *When, later?*

Susan flicked her eyes toward the couple at the altar. *After the wedding.*

Hank acquiesced by returning his attention to the matters at hand.

And just in the nick of time, Susan realized, as the judge turned to them for the rings that the bride and groom were to exchange.

Thankful for the details that demanded their concentration for the rest of the proceedings, Susan performed her duties as matron of honor, breathing a premature sigh of relief at putting her husband off. She had forgotten that once the marriage was official she would have to walk back down the garden path beside the man she herself had married almost fourteen years ago.

Hank didn't forget, however. When Susan hesitated to accept his elbow, he took her hand and tucked it firmly in the crook of his arm before squeezing the heavily muscled limb back against his side. His wife had no doubt that retrieving her hand was going to be a difficult if not impossible task when they reached the back door of Tanner's farmhouse.

"All right," Hank whispered out of the corner of his mouth as they passed the last few rows of folding chairs. "The wedding is over. Let's talk."

"Not yet," Susan told him. "There's still the reception to go."

"But you said—"

"The reception is part of the wedding," his wife insisted. "Now, be quiet. I don't want Lara and Tanner's wedding day spoiled by a fight."

"Who wants to fight? Are you saying—"

"I'm not saying anything until Tanner and Lara leave for their honeymoon."

"But—"

"Hank," she warned him in her best honey-don't-push-me tone of voice.

"Okay, okay. But after the reception we talk."

"I already agreed to that," she reminded him. They joined the newlyweds then and Hank was forced to relinquish his hold on her to shake hands with Tanner.

The groom wasn't offended by his best man's lack of enthusiasm. Thumping Hank soundly on the back, Tanner whispered, "I hope my luck rubs off on you."

Hank shot a grateful look at the other man. "Me too, old son. Me too."

The foursome were torn apart by the crush of well-wishers anxious to congratulate the happy couple. For the next two hours, none of the wedding party was given a chance to do anything other than pose for pictures and agree that "Yes, the wedding was beautiful," and "Yes, they were obviously meant for each other."

Susan and Kelly were kept busy with cups of punch and saucers for cake and rice bags for everyone. When their escorts began to dog their every step, Susan chastised them for neglecting the getaway car until Hank finally left to fulfill his duty, dragging an equally reluctant groomsman behind him.

"What's with you and L.J.?" Susan asked the bridesmaid as soon as the men were out of range. Lara's older brother hadn't left the redhead's side all day. "Is he after you again?"

"Oh, he's just being a pest," her single friend assured her. "He's not serious. He never has been."

"I wouldn't be too sure about that," Susan cautioned. "If he hadn't been serious in high school he would have asked someone else to go to the prom when you refused. L.J. certainly could have had his pick of dates."

"For heaven's sake, Suz!" Kelly exclaimed. "That was a million years ago. I hardly think he's been pining for me all these years."

"You never know," Susan said over her shoulder as she led the way into the kitchen with a stack of dirty plates. "After all, he hasn't even gotten married and I'm sure he's had ample opportunity. There must be some reason he hasn't settled down yet."

"Sure, there is. He's a confirmed bachelor who is content to play the field."

"Sounds like just your type, then. Hasn't that always been your philosophy, too?"

The redhead shook her head. "Not anymore it isn't. Turning thirty has a way of narrowing a woman's field considerably. I've decided that it's time I made the final score and called the dating game quits."

"You're kidding!" Susan gasped in surprise. "Kelly Ryan married? I'll believe it when I see it. Aren't you the woman who's been telling me how much I've been missing during the past fourteen years of marriage? You always made the single life sound such fun."

"I lied a lot."

"Kelly!"

"Okay, I lied a little. Just like you did. I mean, if marriage was as terrific as you said, how come you and Hank are separated?"

"Maybe we won't be much longer."

Kelly carefully set down the tray she almost dropped. "Say that again."

But Kim popped her head around the edge of the kitchen door before her mother could answer. "Come on, Mom, Aunt Kelly. Lara's getting ready to throw the bouquet."

"Oh, boy," Kelly responded with a noticeable lack of enthusiasm.

"Hey, you just said you wanted to get married. It wouldn't hurt to hedge your bets a little. The woman who catches the bouquet is supposed to be the next bride," Susan reminded her friend.

"All right, all right. Come on, Kim. I'll fight you for it." Together, Kelly and Kim dashed off to join the growing throng of anxious available women.

Susan followed at a much slower pace, coming to a halt on the outskirts of the crowd of onlookers.

"Aren't you going to try for it?"

She looked over her shoulder at the dark, tuxedoed man standing behind her. "I'm already married."

"But when the divorce is final . . ."

"Somehow, I don't think it ever will be," she interrupted.

"Does that mean you've decided to take me back? You'll really give me a second chance?" Her husband held his breath, waiting for her answer as if his life depended on it.

Susan considered putting him off again, then relented. They had already been separated far too long. "If you're sure that's what you want."

When Hank tried to take her in his arms, she forestalled him with a firm hand placed against his chest. "This offer is good one time only. I don't care what the problem may be, if you ever walk out on me again, that's it. Understood?"

"Understood." Hank enfolded her tightly. "Believe me, Susan, I'm not going anywhere. I love you, woman. I'm never going to risk losing you again."

His wife held him just as securely. "I don't want to lose you, either, Hank. I love you, too."

They embraced each other, completely oblivious to their surroundings until a roar from the wedding guests reminded them where they were. Turning toward the commotion, Susan spied Lara's bouquet clutched in the hand of the tall redheaded bridesmaid who was waving her prize triumphantly in the air.

"Now, if L.J. can just manage to catch the garter, everything should be perfect," Hank murmured in his wife's ear.

Susan leaned back against his solid chest. "Is he still interested in her, then?"

"Oh, yeah." Hank chuckled. "It seems he's always had an itch that only she can scratch. Personally, I'd love to see him give Kelly a good run. It's high time someone brought that female under control."

"Now, Hank," his wife chided him.

"I know, I know. You and Lara like Kelly just the way she is. But I, along with the rest of Morristown, think she needs a good man to settle her down. L.J. might just be the guy to fill the bill."

"I don't see how he can when he's living on the other side of the state."

"Just wait and see," Hank promised. "If it's there, love will find a way."

Susan tilted her head back to stare at him in open-mouthed surprise. "That sounded more like something Tanner would say. Maybe he's been a good influence on you, after all."

Hank flushed as he realized that his words had been pretty mushy for a former ex-lineman. However, when his wife brushed a butterfly-soft caress across the corner of his mouth, he forgot all about maintaining his tough-guy status.

"I can be just as romantic as McNeil, you know."

"Oh?"

"Damned straight, I can."

"Care to prove it?"

"As a matter of fact, I would, Mrs. Metcalf."

Fortunately, the crowd was being distracted by Tanner's removal of Lara's garter. The flimsy bit of lace went sailing toward the small, unenthusiastic group of confirmed bachelors. L.J. had no trouble snatching the item out of the air. None of the other men dared to challenge his catch.

To the guests' delight, the tall, lean blonde immediately began stalking Kelly with a devilish intent written clearly on his face. The bridesmaid froze for a second like a doe just realizing that her life was in danger; then her instincts took over. Kelly fled for safety, her cheeks glowing the same shade as her glorious crown of hair, as the handsome hunter followed in hot pursuit.

Hank and Susan surfaced just in time to watch the newlyweds take advantage of the distraction to run for their car. By the time the couple got the whipped cream off the door handle and the balloons out of the interior, their loyal followers had discovered their attempted escape and showered the bride and groom with handfuls of rice.

"Nice decorating job," Susan commented as she and her husband watched the leave-taking from Tanner's front porch.

"Thanks," Hank accepted modestly. "We tried our best." Raising their clasped hands, he waved to the pair who were safely ensconced in the car at last.

Tanner signaled back with a thumbs-up sign, nudging his new wife so that she, too, could witness the successful completion of one matchmaking attempt. It was by far the nicest wedding present they had received.

As the McNeils drove off, the wedding guests began to reassemble their parties, retrieving purses, handkerchiefs and children before taking their own leave.

"I've still got the station wagon," Hank said, tucking Susan's hand back into the crook of his arm. "Did you drive over in the Volkswagen?"

"No, it's still at the Jamisons' house. I rode with Lara and Kelly."

"I guess we can all leave together, then." Hank grinned at the thought. He and Susan, together again. It sounded beautiful to him. "Where are Kim and Jake?"

Their children appeared as if magically summoned by their father's words. Their daughter's ready smile grew even wider when she saw her parents standing arm in arm. Their son, however, looked a little confused.

"Let's go home, kids," Hank said.

"You're coming with us?" Kim asked.

"You betcha," her father answered, his grin spreading from ear to ear.

"You mean you're dropping us off?" Jake clarified cautiously.

"No, son. I'm coming home to stay."

"That's right, Jake. We're all going to be together again," Susan added.

"All right!" Kim flung her arms around each parent in turn. "I knew you'd get back together. I just knew it!"

Susan returned her hug, then turned to accept its twin from Jake. Her son put his long skinny arms around her, leaning close to whisper, "Are you sure about this, Mom? Is this what you want?"

"Yes, this is what I want, Jake," his mother assured. "It's what's best for all of us."

"You got one of those hugs for me, son?" Hank asked.

Jake hesitated, then held his hand out to his father. "Will a handshake do?"

Hank met him halfway, clasping his hand in a firm, sure grip. When he made to let go, however, Jake held on. "Just remember," his son warned him, "I got my eye on you. Make sure you don't step out of line this time."

There wasn't a glimmer of humor in the boy's eyes. "I won't, son. You've got my word on that."

"And I'll hold you to it," Jake promised, dead serious.

They walked four abreast to the car—daughter, father, mother, son. Susan used her own body to bridge the slight gap remaining between her two proud men. As he started the station wagon, Hank cast a searching glance at his wife. She smiled bravely back at him.

No second thoughts. At least, Hank hoped that's what she'd meant.

THE METCALFS MADE only one stop on the way home: the Carriage Motel. Hank didn't even turn the car off while he dashed into his room and grabbed the garbage bags he had kept ready to go ever since Valentine's Day.

At home, he unpacked while his family prepared a celebratory feast, then took his seat at the head of the table, anxious to restake his claim as husband and father.

Dinner went smoothly, with Kim chattering enough to keep Jake and Susan's silence from becoming too uncomfortable. Hank couldn't help but notice that the later the hour, the quieter his wife and son became. He was greatly relieved when the kids' bedtime came. He'd concentrate on one Metcalf at a time, starting with his wife.

"Is he going to spend the night?" Jake asked bluntly as his mother began to close his bedroom door.

"Of course, he's spending the night," Susan said. "Your father's home, Jake. Home to stay. Everything is going to be back to normal now."

"Where is he going to sleep?"

"With your mother, that's where," Hank interrupted as he came to a standstill behind his wife. "Any objections?" he added in a tone that indicated there had better not be.

"I guess not," Jake mumbled.

"Good. Sleep tight. We'll see you in the morning."

"Yes, sir."

As Hank pulled the door to behind them, Susan turned to her husband, obviously flustered. "Did you have to be so blunt, Hank? This has been hard for Jake."

"Come to bed and I'll show you how hard it's been for me," he answered.

Susan hung back as he began to move down the hall toward the master bedroom. "It's too early to go to bed. I'm not tired yet."

"Good," he said. "Neither am I." Hank caught her hand and tugged her gently along behind him. "Come on, Suz. It's time to pay up for all the teasing you've been giving me these past few weeks."

Susan hadn't felt this nervous since long before her wedding night. It wasn't that she didn't want to, because she did. Very much, sort of. It was just that she was afraid, which was silly. Hadn't she proven over and over on their dates just how successfully she could arouse her husband?

But then, she reminded herself, arousing Hank had never exactly been a problem. Satisfying him was another matter, though. Maybe teasing the lion hadn't been such a good idea. What if she had created a hunger she couldn't appease?

Unaware of his wife's thoughts, Hank pulled Susan into their room, closing the door behind them and securing it with a definite click as the lock slid into place.

He'd spent too many nights planning for this scene, agonizing over every last detail.

Hank was going to make love to his wife as never before, repaying her for every teasing lick, bite, nip and suck she'd given him over the past few weeks—kiss for kiss, stroke for stroke.

He began with the T-shirt she'd changed into after the wedding, tugging it gently over her head, tossing it on the floor, then sliding his hands around her back to unhook her bra. All his movements were smooth and easy, as if he were trying to reassure a wild thing captured for its own good.

Susan let him take the lead until she felt the firm support of the mattress against her back, taking their weight; then she snapped out of her passive mode and began to take command herself, just as she had that night on the levee.

She slid out of the cage of Hank's arms, winding around, pinning him beneath her as she finished removing his clothes. Then she repeated her success of previous evenings, leading with her hands, following with her lips and tongue.

Hank let himself be carried away, let her carry him up the sudden rise of desire. As he neared the peak, he opened his eyes to capture the view from the top and looked through the haze to find his wife looking back, her eyes unclouded, her gaze sharply focused through the thick plastic lenses of her glasses. All he could think was *Something's wrong*.

He reached up to lift off her glasses, but Susan pulled back out of reach, rocking her body forward. His hands quickly shifted down to grasp her hips, stilling her movements, allowing him to hold on a little longer.

"It's all right," she whispered. "I just want to see you. I want to see your face, watch what you feel."

"Together," he protested. "We're together now. We should *be* together."

"We are together." She leaned forward again, bending from the waist when he wouldn't surrender his hold, smoothing her lips over his. Squeezing, tightening inside. "Feel it?" She posted gently, using the dampening of his palms to ease his grip. "We're together, Hank. Just let go."

Hold back, hold back, he ordered himself. *Not yet. Wait for her. Take her with you. Take her. Take . . .*

Hank moved with the strength of a cyclone. Sudden, unpredictable. Rolling over, turning them upside down, pinning her beneath, invading full force. The pressure building inside. Inside him, yes. Inside her?

The air stilled as he gathered strength, then the deluge began, pouring inside her, drowning him in his own release. He opened his eyes one last time before going under, searching, hoping. *Where was she? Had she come with him?* And then he knew he had entered the torrent alone.

It was ebbing slowly. Susan rocked him soothingly in the wake of it all. Hank heaved great gusts of wind until slowly his breath came back and settled into gentle breezes against her temple. His strength was spent. She held his weight, cradling him in her arms as if he'd been a child frightened by thunder instead of a man who had been as one with the storm.

I'VE LOST HER, he thought, even as she held him. *I've lost her again.*

Something splashed against her face. Susan lifted a hand to his cheek and wiped away the moisture there. "Hank, what's wrong?"

"You wouldn't come with me." He raised his head slowly, meeting her face-to-face. "Why, Susan? Why not? What am I doing wrong?"

"Nothing!"

"It's been like this ever since we split up," Hank complained, propping himself up on his elbows as his strength gradually returned. "You do it *for* me, but not *with* me. You watch, but you won't jump in. How do I get you back, Susan. Really back. What do I have to do to get you to want me again?"

"You don't have to do anything," she insisted. "I do want you. I've always wanted you. I'm not the one who was tempted to try elsewhere."

"Not that again." Hank flopped over on his back. "Are we ever going to be able to put that behind us?"

"I'm trying. It's just..." Susan sighed, pressing against him, laying her head on his shoulder. "It's just that I need to know that I'm the one you want. I couldn't stand to be filling in for someone else, Hank."

"You're not." He put his arms around her, folding her close. One hand tangled in her hair, then the strong fingers gently set the tangles free. "If anything, the opposite would be true. Anyone else would just be standing in for you. Don't you understand?"

"I'm trying," she whispered. "Give me time, Hank. I'm trying."

"I'll give you more than time," Hank promised, tugging gently on her hair until she looked up at him again. "I'll give you everything I have, everything you can bear to take, until you realize that there couldn't possibly be someone else."

He shifted again so that they were lying side by side, arms around each other. "You're all the woman I've ever wanted, Susan. More woman than I ever dreamed of having. Lord knows, more than I ever deserved."

"That's not true." She shoved her hands against his chest, pushing him away in anger, then pulling him back with love. "Hank, I'm the one that took you for granted. Took everything you gave without even saying thank-you."

Susan pressed one finger against his mouth, preventing an interruption. "I was wrong. I told you once that I didn't want a marriage where I had to keep track of who owed whom. It's taken me a while to admit it, but I realize now it's because I knew I was already so deep in debt for all the years you stood by me and supported us. I owe you, Hank."

"For what?" he scoffed. "Getting you pregnant? I was the one who said he'd take the responsibility for protecting you. I screwed up twice. You think you owe me for that?"

"I think we have to share equal credit for Kim and Jake," Susan told him. "I wasn't ignorant, Hank. I knew the risks and I chose to take them, just as you did. The point is that you stood by me."

"That didn't take anything. I already wanted to marry you, remember? If you hadn't been pregnant, you wouldn't have married me."

"I didn't have to, anyway. I had choices, Hank. I chose you." Susan grabbed his chin, holding his shaking head still, forcing him to look at her. "I chose you and I still owe you, for putting me through college, for keeping the kids when I went to class even though you were bone tired from working all day."

"You were working, too," Hank reminded her. "And as for the tuition, I was just trying to make up for the scholarships you had to turn down."

"Giving up those scholarships was my decision," Susan insisted. "Working for the *Gazette* was my choice. You were the one that was forced to take whatever was available to support us."

"So? It worked out okay. Pretty damned good, in fact. Besides, it wasn't as if I had any great plans or anything. Not like you did."

"You must have had some dreams," Susan said.

"You. You were my only dream, Snookums. You were as ambitious as I dared get. Most people, including your folks, would agree that taking you as my wife was higher than I should have aimed."

"They might have then," Susan admitted. "Not now. Believe me, Hank. If I had ever doubted how lucky I've been, this town has taken great pains to set me straight over the past nine months.

"I took you for granted," she confessed. "And I am sorry. It will never happen again. I'll never be able to repay you for everything you've done for me, for everything you've wanted to do. But I'm going to try, Hank. I'm going to try."

15

HANK KNEW SUSAN had it all wrong. Any way it was added up, he knew he still came out on top in their marriage. Hell, just being given a second chance placed him in far greater debt than the government's budget deficit. His only hope was to try to make up the difference in community service.

He figured driving the propane truck placed him way ahead with folks like the Carlsons. In the long run, maybe the powers that be would total his points for good behavior and decide that he'd earned his right to live happily ever after with the woman of his dreams.

"You're a precious man, Hank. That's exactly what I said in my prayers last night," Ethel Van Dowsen told him the next time he made a propane delivery at her house.

"I said, 'Lord, bless that precious man, Hank Metcalf. I know he'll take the time to light my water heater, unlike those six ungrateful children I raised.'"

"Now, Mrs. Van Dowsen, I don't mind you putting in a good word for me, but don't do it at Jed's expense or any of your other children's. If you hadn't raised them so well, they wouldn't have been able to fly so far from the nest."

Hank smiled. "Be a little silly for them to come all the way back here just for a finicky pilot light. Let them save their money so they can fly you out to see them."

"Oh, no. Nobody's getting me on one of those airplanes. My feet haven't left the ground since I set foot on this earth, and I'd just as soon keep it that way."

Since Hank held pretty much the same philosophy himself, he couldn't argue. "Whatever you say, Mrs. Van Dowsen. I'll just get that pilot light going, then you can call Jed and tell him what a good job I did."

He walked through the shotgun-style house to the bathroom, which had been put in where the back porch used to be. It was a stark room with plain fixtures and the hot water tank stood undisguised in the corner.

Hank lay belly-down on the cold linoleum, located the gas valve and the safety button that would interrupt the flow long enough to light the pilot.

It was a simple favor he often performed for customers free of charge. Anything with an Explosive sticker stuck on the side seemed to intimidate most people. Which was probably just as well, Hank thought, since a simple procedure performed by someone without experience could be a mite dangerous, even though it was perfectly safe for a fellow like himself who knew what he was doing.

Just like driving the propane truck, Hank reflected as he pushed the safety button, struck the match and—

Whoom! The flame leaped out at him like dragon's breath, torching his hands and face. He swatted at the monster, driving it back, twisting its neck to choke off the fire. Still he burned. He rolled instinctively across the floor, his scorched hands smothering the sparks in his hair.

A wave washed over him. He was drowning in fire. Was that possible? Not enough prayers, not enough. Hell was hotter than he'd ever imagined. All he could see were flames, sparks dancing in his eyes.

Then angels' wings beat out the fire. "Hank! Oh, Lord, Hank! I'm sorry. I'm sorry. Oh, Lord, help me! What should I do?"

Yes, please, he thought. *Lord help the angel put out the fire. I'll be good. Please. I'll be good. Please! I don't need heaven yet, just let me go home. Please, just let me go home! Susan . . .*

Fluffy clouds, soft as pillows. The flames were gone though the heat remained. The angel whispered in his ear. "Gotta get help. Time's a-wasting. Better not wait. Come on, Hank. Come on, son. You're too big to carry. Get up. Get up. Takes too long to get here. Gotta go. Let's go."

"MRS. METCALF?"

Susan nearly jumped into the doctor's arms. "Is he okay, Dr. Price? Will Hank be all right?"

"Relax. He's fine," Dr. Price assured her. "We're going to keep him in the hospital overnight just to be sure. The burns don't look that serious, although we can't say definitely until tomorrow. Just flash burns probably. Still, they can be quite painful, and any burn carries the risk of infection."

Susan nodded, absorbing the diagnosis with relief. "Can I see him now?"

"Certainly. Hank's in Room 113, straight down the hall on the left. We've given him something for the pain, so don't be surprised if he seems a little out of it when you talk to him."

His eyebrows had been singed off, but they'd grow back, the nurses assured her. The yellowish glaze coating the angry red burns was just medication. Nothing to worry about. He was going to be fine.

"Hank?" She called his name softly, not wanting to wake him if he was already asleep.

His lashless lids lifted a bit, and bloodshot eyes peered through narrow slits. "Susan?"

"I'm right here, honey." She started to take his hand, then realized it was burned, too. Her fingers wrapped around the bed rail instead. "How do you feel? Is there anything I can do for you?"

He moved his head slightly, rustling the sheets. "No."

"Bill Price is the one who treated you. He says you're going to be just fine."

Hank closed his eyes again. "Tired. Sorry."

"It's okay," she told him. "We'll talk later. I'll be right here when you wake up."

"Kids?" he whispered.

"They're at my mother's. Worried, of course, but I already told them you were going to be fine. Just flash burns, probably."

Hank was asleep before she'd finished speaking. The medication had taken hold, dragging him away from consciousness. Susan knew it was for the best. He would feel less pain that way.

She sat down in the chair by his bed, leaning her head back, watching diligently for any signs of distress. His injuries weren't life threatening. She knew that. Still, it didn't hurt to be careful.

What if he'd been killed? What if it had all ended? She couldn't help but think of all the months they had wasted—months that could have been spent together.

But they weren't wasted, she told herself sternly. They had learned from them. Things were better. Susan knew that was true, in spite of the gut feeling she had that the reunification hadn't been a complete success. It felt, sometimes, as if they were still missing a piece or two of the puzzle, as if there were small gaps waiting to trip them up.

Weak spots, that's what they were, Susan thought. Like the leak in the roof Hank had noticed on Valentine's Day. A little thing that, left untreated, could become a big problem. That's what had been bothering her. She and Hank hadn't patched all their leaks yet.

She watched the even rise and fall of his chest. Thank heavens, they still had time. Thank heavens it had been a water-heater valve that had malfunctioned instead of that damned propane truck he insisted on driving.

That's where she'd start repairs, Susan decided. It shouldn't be that difficult. Surely this accident would make Hank see the light. Driving that truck was too risky for a married man. She'd told him that before, but he hadn't listened.

Hank liked getting out of the office. He liked visiting the farms, talking to his friends, seeing the S&S inventory put to use, getting feedback on what his clients wanted.

Well, he could do a door-to-door survey in his pickup if that's what he wanted. She'd be damned if he'd get back behind that propane truck's wheel again.

"How is he?"

Susan jerked her head toward the doorway. "Hank's fine, Mrs. Van Dowsen. Don't worry. They're just holding him overnight for safekeeping."

"As they should," the older woman said. "He's a national treasure, that one." Mrs. Van Dowsen patted the pockets of her housedress, searching for a tissue.

"Here." Susan handed her one from the box on Hank's nightstand.

"Oh, thank you, dear." The woman settled her rotund body into the other chair. "I haven't been able to stop blubbering ever since it happened. I feel so bad, sugar. It was all my fault. I shouldn't have been taking up his time, anyway. My son told me I needed to have that water heater replaced, but I didn't believe him. They should lock me up, they should. Serve me right. Tried to save a nickel and nearly cost a man's life."

"It's all right, Mrs. Van Dowsen. You couldn't have known the safety would malfunction. The important thing is that Hank's all right. I'm grateful to you for getting him here so fast."

"Oh, it was the least I could do. The very least. I thought about calling them para-whachits but it would have taken them forever just to get out to the farm. My son's right, you know. I really should move into town. He's got this little apartment complex for older folks in mind. It's a nice place, really. I know I should go. But the farm's my home, you understand. It hurts just to think about leaving it."

"I know." Susan smiled sympathetically, allowing Mrs. Van Dowsen to ramble on until Hank's partners, Buddy and Joe, rushed into the room.

"Is he going to be all right, Susan? Is there anything we can do?"

Susan almost shook her head "No" before she realized that these two were just the men she needed. "As a matter of fact there is, Joe. Come on outside where we can talk." She followed the men into the hallway, looking back over her shoulder to make sure Hank was still asleep.

"Oh, you go right ahead, hon," Mrs. Van Dowsen said. "I've got my eye on him. Joe, you and Buddy take her down to the cafeteria and make her eat a bite. She'll be here all night, I'm sure. It won't do to have them both sickly."

"We'll do that, Ethel," Joe Camden promised. "Keep an eye on our boy, there."

"I will, I will."

By the time Susan made it back to his room, ten more people had arrived to take their turn beside Hank's bed. Five of them were contemporaries of Mrs. Van Dowsen. At first, Susan wasn't sure if they were there to see Hank or if they had just moved their quilting bee to the hospital for Ethel Van Dowsen's sake. The ladies quickly put Susan's doubts to rest, echoing Mrs. Van Dowsen's praises.

"You married a precious man, sugar," Mrs. Van Dowsen told her when the group of older women finally began to take their leave. "I hope you know that."

"Yes, Mrs. Van Dowsen, I do." *Precious?* Susan grinned. Somehow that wasn't the sort of adjective one usually associated with a man who'd been called Hank the Tank in his football days.

When Hank woke up the next morning he thought for a moment that he had died and been placed on display for those who wished to pay respects. The roomful of flowers bore a distinct resemblance to Curtner's Funeral Home when it was all decked out for a dead VIP.

Then his nervous system suddenly realized that the painkillers had worn off and Hank knew, without a doubt, that he was still very much alive.

"Morning, Precious," Susan greeted him.

If it had been possible to turn any redder, Hank would have. "I gather Mrs. Van Dowsen's been by."

"Yep. So have all the other ladies in her sewing club." Susan tsked softly. "And to think I was worried about one ex-cheerleader when you've had a dozen femmes fatales dangling on the side."

The fact that she could joke about Sandra Kellogg shocked Hank. And pleased him. For the first time since he had moved back home, he began to relax. Everything was going to be fine.

IT WASN'T UNTIL one week later that Hank realized he had relaxed a little too soon. He came home from his first day back at work furious.

Susan was standing on the front porch when he pulled into the drive. No doubt Joe and Buddy, her co-horts, had phoned to warn her, Hank thought. He got out slowly and approached his wife with the precise movements of a stalking cat. "What the hell are you trying to pull?"

"I'm not trying to pull anything." Susan stood firm, betraying not a shred of the fear she felt. "A woman has the right to protect her husband."

"And a man has a right to support his family in the best way he can."

"Not if it jeopardizes his life," she said. "Besides, driving that propane truck hasn't been part of your job in years. You shouldn't have gotten back behind that wheel in the first place."

"I don't tell you how to run your newspaper," Hank said. "So don't tell me how to run my business."

"It's Joe and Buddy's business, too," Susan reminded him. "And they agreed with me."

Hank shook his finger in her face. "That's another thing I want to talk to you about. What the hell gives you the right to go behind my back and talk to my partners?"

Susan held up her left hand, her gold wedding band gleaming on her ring finger. "This gives me the right, Hank. This, plus the fact that I love you. Can't you understand how I felt seeing you in the hospital like that, fried to a crisp?"

"But the truck didn't have a damned thing to do with the accident," Hank said. "You're being irrational. That's not like you, Suz. A safety button on a water heater malfunctions, so you want me to quit driving a fuel truck. Can't you see there's no connection?"

His wife shook her head. "All I can see every time I close my eyes is a coffin filled with ashes. You know how I feel about you driving that truck, Hank."

"You know how I feel about the *Gazette*, but I don't see you giving it up."

"Now who's being irrational?" Susan asked. "Publishing the *Gazette* certainly isn't life threatening."

"No, but it sure has been a big financial risk. Not to mention the time it consumes," Hank countered. "In its own way, the newspaper had been just as big a threat to the family's security as my driving that propane truck."

Susan gasped as the light began to dawn. "Is that why you're still doing it? To get back at me?"

"Hell no!" Hank thrust his hands into the pockets of his jeans. "Look, Susan. We've been through this all before. I told you that I just like getting out and seeing everyone. And it's good for business. You saw how many people came to visit me in the hospital. You saw all the flowers."

"Yes, I saw," she admitted. "And I wasn't surprised when I heard about all the things you've been doing for them."

"But don't you understand, then?" Hank asked. "Those people need me. Sure, we could hire another driver. But is he going to light a water-heater pilot for an old widow? Or sit for a spell with the housebound folks like Red Carlson? I can't stop driving the truck now, Susan. Those people have started depending on me."

He stepped closer, his hands gently closing around her upper arms. "Don't you understand? *They* need me."

"And you think I don't?"

Hank grunted. "You used to. When you were pregnant. When the kids were small. Maybe even when you started the *Gazette*. But you haven't needed me in a long time, Susan. The past year has proven that. You got along just fine without me."

"I survived," Susan corrected him. "Because I had to. But I sure wouldn't say everything was fine."

"But you didn't need me," Hank said again in a hushed, mournful tone. "You don't need me anymore."

"Oh, Hank." Susan cradled his thick-skulled head between her palms. "Is that what this whole thing has been about? Is that why you really left me last year? You think I don't need you anymore?"

He lowered his eyes, seeming ashamed of his inadvertent confession. Susan clucked her tongue at her own foolishness. *This was it—the damned spot that hadn't been fixed.* She pushed up on her toes and stroked her lips across his mouth. "Oh, Hank. You'd probably die of stress if you knew how much I need you."

She leaned against him, smiling when Hank automatically shifted his stance in order to support their combined weight. "Do you know why I married you, Hank?"

"Sure. You were pregnant."

"Uh-uh." Again her lips brushed against his as she gently shook her head. "That's not why."

Hank pulled back and stared at her, clearly confused. "But you turned me down when I asked you to marry me. You didn't change your mind until after you found out about Kim."

Susan smiled. "Hank, I knew I was pregnant when you proposed."

"You knew? But then why didn't you say yes the first time?"

"Because I knew what the odds were against teenage marriages. I didn't want us to end up like so many of the other couples we knew."

Hank cocked his head to one side and studied her dubiously. "What made you change your mind?"

"What you said. Remember? You told me that no one could ever love me as much as you."

"I meant it," he said. "I still think it's the truth."

"So do I." Susan kissed him again. "That's why I finally said yes. That's why I said yes again. Because I've always known no one could ever love me like you do.

"*That's* what I need from you, Hank," she continued. "That's what I've always needed. Financial support, a good father for my children, fabulous sex—those are all extras. Your love is the only thing that was essential. The one thing that I'll always need and only you can give."

Hank crushed his arms around her, lifting Susan clear off the ground. "Oh, baby. You don't know how much I needed to hear that."

"There's something else you should know, Henry Jacob Metcalf, Sr.," Susan said when her feet finally touched down again.

"Yes?"

"It works both ways." Her gaze locked with his, leaving no room for doubt. "No one could ever love you as much as I do." She grinned then, poking a finger in his chest. "So, don't ever get it in your head to go looking elsewhere. Understand?"

"Yes, Snookums."

"And that's another thing. I thought we agreed you weren't to call me Snookums anymore."

"But you didn't like any of the alternatives I suggested."

"You mean Poopsie and Fido? You can't be serious. That's taking pet names a bit too literally."

Hank shrugged. "Obviously we're not going to agree on this. Why don't we try another topic?"

"Such as?"

"I believe I heard something about fabulous sex."

Susan smiled. "Did I mention that?"

"Yes, you did," he assured her. "And I think that's definitely something we need to discuss in depth."

"Oh, really?"

"Yeah." Hank lifted Susan up into his arms, kicked the front door open and carried his wife over the threshold. "I think that's an excellent place to begin again."

Then he turned toward the stairs and found his way blocked by two grinning adolescents. Hank sighed, slowly letting his wife slide down till she was standing on her own two feet.

The couple shared a wry smile as Susan put her arm around his waist, leaned close and said, "Welcome home, *precious*. Welcome home."

CHRISTMAS
STORIES · 1991

Bring back heartwarming memories of Christmas past
with HISTORICAL CHRISTMAS STORIES 1991,
a collection of romantic stories
by three popular authors.
The perfect Christmas gift!

Don't miss these heartwarming stories,
available in November
wherever Harlequin books are sold:

CHRISTMAS YET TO COME
by Lynda Trent
A SEASON OF JOY
by Caryn Cameron
FORTUNE'S GIFT
by DeLoras Scott

**Best Wishes and Season's Greetings
from Harlequin!**

XM-91R

HARLEQUIN
Romance

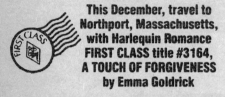

**This December, travel to
Northport, Massachusetts,
with Harlequin Romance
FIRST CLASS title #3164,
A TOUCH OF FORGIVENESS
by Emma Goldrick**

Folks in Northport called Kitty the meanest woman in town,
but she couldn't forget how they had duped her brother and
exploited her family's land. It was hard to be mean, though,
when Joel Carmody was around—his calm, good humor
made Kitty feel like a new woman. Nevertheless, a Carmody
was a Carmody, and the name meant money and power to
the townspeople.... Could Kitty really trust Joel, or was he
like all the rest?

Harlequin Temptation dares to be different!

Once in a while, we Temptation editors spot a romance that's truly innovative. To make sure *you* don't miss any one of these outstanding selections, we'll mark them for you.

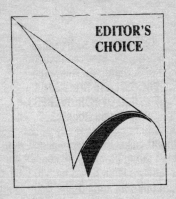

EDITOR'S CHOICE

When the "Editor's Choice" fold-back appears on a Temptation cover, you'll know we've found that extra special page-turner!

THE

Temptation

EDITORS